STUBBORN LOVE

THE STUBBORN LOVE SERIES

WENDY OWENS

ORANGEWILLOW PUBLISHING

* * *

This one is for my daughter Zoe. You may have been a baby but you were there for me every step of the way as I figured out who I was and what really mattered.

The road to finding love is a bumpy one.
From a girl who struggled with closing off her own heart and managed to still find true love, this book was a journey of self-exploration.

SERIES NOTE

The Stubborn Love Series consists of stories about the tough journey of the heart. They are companion novels and do not have to be read together to understand each story. All books focus on a different couple. Love isn't always easy and often can be painful, but if we open our hearts the rewards can be endless.

*Did you realize all the Stubborn Love Series book titles are inspired by songs?

STUBBORN LOVE

ONLY IN DREAMS

THE LUCKIEST

NEWSLETTER SIGNUP

Would you like a FREE short story? Do you want to make sure you don't miss any upcoming releases or giveaways? Be sure to sign up for my newsletter at http://signup.wendyowensbooks.com/

PROLOGUE

I looked at him, sitting there, head drooped over in his hands, sobbing like a child, but I had no sympathy left in me to give. I had been going through this cycle with him for too long now. I knew all the tricks he would play all too well. First was anger; his temper would flare when I didn't do what he wanted. He would use that fury to try and control me. In the beginning, I believed the awful things he said to me and accepted them as truth. Over time, though, I began to see Ashton for what he was—a bully.

He was used to me falling right in line. My rebellious streak as of late showed me new glimpses of just how terrible he could be. When his tactics seemed to no longer work on me I began to see his anger boil over. This darker side of him terrified me.

Over the years I had lost track of the outbursts, broken furniture, holes in walls and, even on the rare occasion, the bruises. I knew, overall, Ashton wasn't a monster, which was perhaps why I stuck it out so long. He was a spoiled little boy who didn't know how to handle his emotions when he didn't get his way.

We met in high school, when a girl's self esteem was typically on a roller coaster, based on what peers thought and said. Ashton was the gorgeous bad boy who I had no business being with. I was the quiet girl, always in the art wing, avoiding large groups of people. It wasn't that I didn't like people; I simply didn't understand them—all of the cliques: jocks, preppies, skaters, cheerleaders, metal heads, even farm kids. I didn't understand the point of segregating like that. Looking back, I supposed I was doing the same thing.

I was part of a much smaller group, though. It was just my best friend, Laney, and me. We had been friends since grade school. She was a bigger girl who constantly obsessed about her weight. I learned to ignore this annoying habit since she was the only real friend I had, that is, until Ashton.

I still remember the day he first spoke to me. He had on a pair of washed-out blue jeans and a plain white v-neck t-shirt. His long, sandy-colored hair hung in his face, with much more stubble than a boy his age should have had. He was the type of boy that would send fathers running for their shotguns; luckily for him, mine wasn't around anymore. I was in the phase of life where thrift store cardigans and oversized denim overalls, matched with a pair of scuffed Doc Martens, somehow seemed fashion appropriate.

"Seven Nation Army" by The White Stripes played in my headphones that day as I felt a tug on one of my pigtails. Spinning on my heel, expecting to see Laney, I was shocked when instead I laid eyes on him. With a half-smile on his lips, he was clearly pleased by my reaction.

Tugging on one of the headphones, I raised an eyebrow in confusion, but said nothing. I couldn't speak. There was no reason in the world I could imagine for this guy to be speaking to me. He was beautiful—a specimen for all teen girls to behold. His shoulder-length hair made me want to reach out and twist it around my finger while I gazed into his hazel eyes. He seemed to always be looking for the opportunity to take off his shirt around school, and a glimpse of what his muscular torso looked like flashed into my mind. I even shocked myself when, for a brief moment, I wondered what his full lips might taste like.

I knew him, or rather, of him. I knew in junior high he went through a skater phase. I knew he dated most of the girls in our class by the time he was in high school and was now moving on to college girls. I also knew there was no way he could possibly be tugging on my pigtail. I was nothing—invisible to most. The outside of my hands were always stained with smudges of graphite, my unkempt wiry hair often spattered with bits of paint. I wasn't ugly. I was aware of that, even then, but I was certain I was nothing special. Nobody to be noticed.

"Clementine, right?"

I remember I cringed when he asked me my name. My mother was also an artist and a bit of a free spirit. She was the only one who called me by my given name. Though I hated it, I never fought her on it. I always worried my dad leaving us was too much on her, so I was careful to never upset her.

"I go by Emmie," I answered. I never understood what drew his interest to me that day. I'd asked him before, and he claimed he always noticed me, but had only then worked up enough courage to ask me out. I knew him well enough to know that was a lie.

That was the moment—the turning point—I began to change. The more time I spent with him, the more he planted ideas in my head. My hair would look better this way instead, or why didn't I ever wear clothes to show off my curves. I was a teenage girl; what was I to do?

Laney was the first to say something to me about the difference, but it had just made me angry. I finally had this amazingly hot guy showing interest in me, and she had to come along and try to ruin it. Ashton explained she was just jealous. Eventually, Laney reached a point where she felt forced to do something. She came to me like a good friend, pointed out that since Ashton came along I didn't care about anything, not even my art. She gave me a choice: it was she or Ashton. I missed her, but I was sure I would always have Ashton.

Fast forward and there I was. The idea of always having Ashton made my skin crawl. I tried to free myself from him a few times, but he was like a bog that pulled you back in, suffocating you. When I was eighteen I told Ashton I was leaving. I was certain I wasn't meant to stay in a small town, and I wanted him to come with me to art school in New York.

He had no intention, however, of ever leaving our sleepy-eyed town. He was the only child of one of the richest couples in the county, so as long he stayed, he would never have to grow up or ever be responsible. Small town rich was quite different than what most people thought of when it came to being wealthy. For us, though, and our small piece of the world, it was rich just the same.

I mustered up as much courage as I could gather and left for New York alone. I managed to stay away five whole days. When the reality sank in that I was alone in a huge city, with no friends, no job, no family, and no plan —except that I wanted to be an artist—I panicked. Ashton was waiting for me when I got off the bus. It was raining. He told me he forgave me.

I enrolled in the local college, and we were married the following spring. His mother told me that she had never seen her son so happy. I decided a small town life with him was better than any other kind of life without him. I was so naive.

The first year was actually pretty good. I went to school while Ashton helped out at his family insurance business a couple days a week. His dad decided that was enough work to justify a full-time salary. The phrase "boys will be boys," became a common theme around the Stirling estate. Ashton was happy with the arrangement so I didn't say anything; after all, when Ashton was happy, everyone was happy. Then everything fell apart.

The economy shifted, everyone tightened their belts, and within six months, Ashton's parents went from the wealthiest in town to nearly broke. Ashton told me not to worry; he would find a new job. He worked at a pizza place for a half day, but it was beneath him. Then there was the video rental store; he made it one full day there. He couldn't hold a job because he was never designed to follow someone's orders. I told him I would take a leave from college until he could find a job that made him happy. I never went back.

"I swear, Em, if you leave me I'll kill myself," Ashton said looking up at me, his hair sticking to his damp cheeks.

"Don't make this any harder than it needs to be," I replied, confident his threats were empty, a desperate and sad attempt to manipulate me.

"I'm not kidding, I'll do it! I can't live without you," Ashton pleaded.

I balled my fingers tightly into small fists, the anger welling up intensely inside me. I wasn't mad at him, though, somewhere in the back of my mind I told myself, it seemed like he meant it this time. I gritted my teeth, focusing on every time he lost a job, every violent fit of rage, every time he would stagger home drunk at four in the morning and pass out on the lawn. Every time he was sorry, he would never do it again, he couldn't lose me. *You can do this.*

"Ashton, do what you have to do, and I'll do what I have to. Goodbye." I turned to walk away. I knew if I stood there looking at his pathetic but handsome face any longer I wouldn't be able to resist him. I would fall back into his arms and tell him how much I loved him. I would try to fix him again.

Ashton couldn't love anyone more than he loved himself, and I needed to get away while there was still enough of me left to salvage.

I opened the door and took that first liberating step onto the tiny landing of our suburban ranch home. Pulling the door closed behind me, it felt like I was closing the door on my past, on my history of dysfunction and cycle of abuse. There was no doubt in my mind that I loved Ashton—he had been my world for all of my short adult life. That was the problem: he was everything. When he said I looked fat or ugly, I felt it; I would begin to see that staring back at me in the mirror. When he told me I was lucky he actually stuck around, I convinced myself I was.

When his temper became violent I even had excuses for that. Ashton would never hit me. He takes it out on the stuff around him because he loves me so much. Then when it escalated and the temper turned on me I somehow managed to justify that, as well. He didn't mean it… I know better than to get in his way when he's like that.

I can't pinpoint the moment it started to change. I suppose a person can only be beaten down for so long before they begin to yearn for their spirit to be set free. I tried telling Ashton that I needed more. I didn't want to work in a bank. I wanted to be an artist. I wanted to follow my dreams, and I wanted more than anything for him to treat me like he loved me.

Don't get me wrong; sometimes he could be a real sweetheart, saying all the perfect things. He was always quick to spend the money I earned on flowers for me. Especially when he wanted something, he could really lay on the charm. The mean streak didn't come out until he didn't get his way.

Taking several steps out into the yard, I kicked off my flip-flops, allowing my toes to sink into the lush green grass, curling them tightly and then flexing them outward. A deep breath filled my lungs before I exhaled. This was it: this was what freedom felt like. I'll admit, I was scared as hell, and I didn't know what being alone looked like, but I was ready for the experience.

I turned back and looked at the door to the home where I thought my life would always be. I had half expected Ashton to chase me outside, making a scene in front of all the neighbors, begging me not to go. I was surprised he didn't. I think he knew as much as I did, this time, I wasn't changing my mind. This time, no amount of screaming or crying would make me stay.

"Bye Ash—" I whispered, just before the shot filled my ears. Echoing and ricocheting around my head for a few moments, the sound caused me to tremble. My head started to rock slightly from side to side, my eyes filling with tears, I couldn't move—frozen to the spot where my bare feet were planted in that lush grass. I just stood, staring at the door, telling myself I hadn't heard the noise I knew I just had.

My neighbor, Bill Peterson, appeared before me. He had shown up on moving day a couple years ago, the second the truck pulled up, like a stray dog searching for a friend. He had introduced himself, pointed out his nearby home with the perfectly manicured lawn, and helped us carry in every single box. I think he was impressed to have a Stirling living next door. The invites to cookouts and other random events seemed endless. Ashton was always game, even if I was exhausted from a long day at work. I would always smile and make small talk with Peterson's wife.

I could tell Bill was saying something to me, but I couldn't hear him. The last thing I had heard was the gunshot, and then nothing but ringing. Bill began waving his arms in front of my face, but I couldn't look away. I just continued staring at the front door of our home.

Throwing up his arms, I watched Bill turn and run toward the house, pushing open the front door. I didn't follow... *couldn't* follow. Tilting my head to one side, I simply continued to stare. Minutes passed before Bill stumbled from our home, his hands covered in blood, frantically dialing a phone.

Only then did I move. Only when I saw his hands, was the spell broken. I fell to my knees, sighing. I was so close, I could taste the freedom, but I should have known. Ashton would never let me get away so easily. A tear rolled down my cheek, a flash shot through my mind of Ashton sitting, sobbing, and pleading with me. I thought twenty-three would be the year I reclaimed my identity. Ashton decided to give me a new one. Widow. A woman so cold she could drive her husband to suicide.

hree Years Later...

The blaring noise of the car horns surrounded me, causing the hair on my arms to stand up straight, as if it were my 'spidey sense.' I had only been in the city for a couple of weeks, and I wasn't used to the constant chaos that seemed to surround me here. If I had my choice, I would have stayed with my mom in Indiana.

We moved there together after Ashton—well, just after. Mom had friends, from what she referred to as her 'younger years,' who lived on a hippie commune called The Grove. She loathed when I would call it a commune, arguing that just because a group of like-minded people decided to live together, working toward the betterment of each other's lives, didn't make the place a commune. Instead, she called it 'a community of enlightened individuals.'

I should have thanked her; in a way, The Grove saved my life. The people there kept their distance, unlike back in Ohio, where I couldn't walk down the street without someone asking me if I was all right, or if there was something they could do for me. It made me want to scream at the top of my lungs, "No you idiot, I'm not okay. My husband just blew his brains out, and it's all my fault." Instead, I smiled, playing the role of grieving widow as best I could.

The Grove was full of other broken people, just like me. Instead of questions, they simply offered acceptance. I was able to keep to myself, and some days I managed to get away without even seeing another living soul, besides my mother, of course. I managed to develop a routine. My mom would go to local markets and fairs with residents of our tiny community, selling goods they created. After a while, she offered to take some of my paintings to sell. It didn't take long before I developed a following. I even started selling my work online, which allowed me to start a nice little savings account for myself.

When the day came for me to leave Indiana, my mom pointed out I had the same anxieties when I left the place that had been home for my entire life. She was right, though I could never tell her that because I was far too stubborn. The funeral had been hard. His dad kept pushing for answers, wanting to know what would have driven his son to such an end. I couldn't tell him. How could I tell his father he lost his only child because of me —because I was leaving Ashton? I pushed him past his breaking point. I did this.

The entire burial process had been quite overwhelming for me. I went from the mindset that I was leaving Ashton, to planning all the details of his funeral.

Once he was gone, it didn't seem right to tell everyone what we had been going through. Nobody needed to know how messed up our relationship was; that would be my burden to carry now. I couldn't figure out if I was pissed at him for doing this to me or at myself for what I had done to him.

The funeral week was a blur: what color casket, would you like a single tombstone or couples, will there be a wake with food? The questions were endless; at least Ashton took the decision of open or closed casket out of the equation. His closest friends put together a tribute video for the service and gave touching speeches about what an amazing man he was, including how much he loved me. It was complete bull. They carried the casket while his favorite R.E.M. song, "Find The River," played in the background; I surprised even myself when I cried.

At first, everyone treated me like I was a wounded animal; they wanted to help me, protect me, and nurse me back to health. As time passed, things changed. They looked at me differently, and perhaps it was my own paranoia, but I think most of them figured I might as well have pulled the trigger. Who knows, maybe they were right?

My mom could see what was happening, the way the small town rumor mill was beginning to wear on me. I couldn't stay in the house where Ashton had ended things. After the funeral, I handed the keys over to his father, as he had mostly paid for the home, and there was no possible way I could handle the process of selling it. It didn't take me long to become somewhat of a hermit. I had suddenly become the girl who only left the house to go to work. A little more time passed, and I couldn't even bring myself to go to work.

When my mom first told me she wanted us to move, I fought her. I told her I couldn't leave. Honestly, I think part of me felt like I deserved the pain the town wanted to inflict on me. It didn't take much pushing, though; I had very little fight left in me at that point.

I'll never forget those first couple weeks at The Grove. I started going out of my mind. Ashton haunted my dreams—he was everywhere I looked. I didn't know what to do. I changed my name back from Stirling to my maiden name, Hayes, in an attempt to regain a portion of my identity. Mom was the one who convinced me to pursue my studies through a distant learning program. It was the first thing she had suggested that made sense to me. I needed something to bury myself in—a distraction.

And it worked. I completed everything I could on my degree via correspondence in record time and still managed to find time to paint. Of course, it helped that mom refused to have a television when we moved. She claimed she was tired of all the negativity the rest of the world had to offer. It was shocking how much time the device had eaten up in the past.

Once I completed my correspondence courses I was left with a choice: I could accept a degree in art history and be done with it; or, if I wanted the fine arts degree that I had always aspired to earn, I would need to go to a physical university to complete my studio courses. If I buckled down, and worked hard, I knew I could finish in a year.

Applying was the easy part, though. I never thought I

would actually get into either of the two schools I'd applied to. It is very easy to say you want something that might be scary, when deep down you think it is impossible. Courage comes from actually following through when the opportunity presents itself. An education primarily made up of distance learning, a patchy portfolio, at best, and the fact that I was now twenty-six years old, I was certain of the response I would receive. But then, if I applied, at least I could say I tried, and no one would ever be able to tell me I didn't.

As part of the application process I was required to write an essay as to why I deserved one of the few spots available to Parsons School of New Design. I don't actually remember writing the paper. That sometimes happened to me. Stuff about Ashton seemed to get put into boxes in my mind, tucked away onto dusty shelves, never to be thought about again. When the acceptance letter arrived, it said the essay had clenched it for me. I considered pulling it out and rereading what words had managed to open this door for me, but thought better of delving into those dusty boxes.

Which leads me to now. It was that quick. I had managed to build a quiet existence of solitude in the past few years, and now... now I was surrounded by chaos.

I thought finding an apartment would be easy; I was never so wrong about anything... well, except maybe for Ashton all those years ago? Classes started in two days, and though I had seen about thirty units, I was no closer to finding a place to live than the day I started. Though I had been saving money, it was quickly becoming evident that what I thought would be a nice sum to live on for a year, was nothing compared to the cost of living in New York.

"Are you getting in or not?" asked an impatient voice behind me.

I turned around to see the most ornately decorated girl I had ever laid eyes on. Her hair was pulled up into a tight ponytail on top of her head, pink stripes randomly placed throughout her platinum blonde hair. Her dress was a white retro cut A-line, adorned with cutout lace flowers. Climbing up both arms were brightly colored bracelets, and her four-inch red patent leather shoes caused her to tower over my five foot eight inch frame.

"I'm sorry?" I asked, confused by what she was asking.

Placing a hand on her hip, clearly annoyed, she clarified, "The taxi. You've had your hand on the door for the past five minutes. Are you getting in or not?"

"Oh—" Startled, I looked down and realized I had zoned out. This happened to me sometimes, as well. "I was headed to West 16th Street."

"I didn't ask your life story, hon."

I looked at the girl, my face burning bright red. "Sorry."

"Are you a nut job?" the girl inquired, giving my body the elevator look. I glanced down at myself, my bohemian skirt seemed to be hanging properly, my v-neck t-shirt had a stain from breakfast, but nothing I thought seemed too offensive.

"I don't understand... What do you mean?" I questioned, looking back to the girl's sparkling blue eyes.

"I have a shoot in the Meatpacking District. We can split the cab if you're not a crazy."

Remembering my quickly dwindling funds, I decided the idea had merit. Nodding, I climbed in, the slender blonde following me. We each gave our addresses to the cabbie.

"I'm Paige." As the girl introduced herself I felt a wave of disappointment wash over me. Not that there was anything wrong with her name, but I had imagined something so much more exotic; perhaps Keira or Delphine.

"Clementine, but my friends call me Emmie," I responded with a smile.

"Well, since I don't really know you, I'll call you Clementine," Paige chimed, looking out the window.

Something was off about Paige, but I liked whatever it was. She was snarky. I could see how her humor could easily be mistaken for rudeness.

"So, where are you from?" she inquired, glancing in my direction.

Surprised she had so quickly made me for a tourist, I asked, "How do you know I'm not a New Yorker?"

"Please, I grew up here, the last thing you are is one of us. Not a bad thing, sweetheart, but I can spot a tourist a mile away."

"I'm not a tourist," I corrected her. "Not exactly. I'm moving here from Ohio, well, Indiana, to go to art school."

"Which is it? Ohio or Indiana?"

I smiled. Paige was quick witted, which I liked. "I grew up in Ohio, but moved to Indiana a couple years ago."

"Welcome hayseed," Paige offered, before leaning forward and tapping on the cabbie's window. "Come on! Do I look like an idiot?"

17

The man mumbled something under his breath before taking a sharp turn down a side street.

"You gotta watch some of these guys. They'll take the highest traffic routes to jack up the fare on you," Paige explained.

"I see, thank you," I replied, taking note of her warning.

"Don't get me wrong—most are honest—just saying, not all of them are, ya know?"

I nodded, but I didn't know. I felt like I didn't know much. Twenty-six years old, and all I seemed to understand was pain.

"Art school, huh?" Paige asked, which I assumed was her attempt at small talk.

Happy to not think about my past, or the pain I was trying to escape, I gladly engaged in the conversation. "Yeah, Parsons."

"No shit?" Paige said, squinting and looking closely at me. "You a transfer student or something?"

I smiled. This girl said what she thought, and I liked that, too. She could tell I wasn't fresh out of high school anymore. "Yeah, I needed to get my senior studios in. I've been looking at apartments, but no luck yet. I knew it was expensive out here, but I had no idea it was this insane. I'm still waiting on my living stipend from school to show up, too."

I could see Paige's ears perk up when she heard that I was receiving a stipend for living expenses.

"Do you mind roommates?" she asked quickly.

"No, I mean, not as long as I have my own space to work," I answered. Based on the prices of the places I was finding, this was a much taller order than I had originally anticipated.

Paige reached over and grabbed the pencil that was resting inside the spiral casing at the top my sketchpad. Pulling it free, she scribbled a number on the front. "We might have a spot opening up in our loft."

Just the sound of it—loft—it was so elegant, and so New York. "All right, I will, I mean—call you."

A moment of silence lingered between us before my curiosity got the better of me. "So, are you a model or something? I mean, I don't want to be nosey, but you said you had a shoot to get to."

"No, I just like to dress up like Rainbow Brite for fun," Paige answered with a serious face.

"Well, I like your look," I said, unsure if I had offended her.

"You've got to be kidding me? This crap is so uncomfortable. These low budget jobs are incredibly annoying, but money is money, right?"

"Yeah, I guess." But I really had no idea what she was talking about. A low budget job versus a high budget—they both seemed glamorous to me.

"Some club is trying to act like they're the new hip rave scene, and I get to go to a shoot and pretend to actually be having fun." Paige stuck her finger down her throat to mimic a gagging motion.

"So—I take it's not a cool place to go?"

"If you have to advertise you're underground, then you're about as far from underground as one can get. The wankers pay cash, so oh well."

I had never actually heard anyone use the term

'wanker,' but I wished I could use it and sound as cool, however, I already knew I could not.

The cab screeched to a sudden halt. "150 West 16th Street." Glancing at the total on the meter, I handed the cabbie my share and stepped out onto the street.

Paige leaned over before I closed the door, and inspecting the dingy street, she giggled then added, "I'll expect your call."

"Nice meeting you," I said with a smile. The moment the door was closed, the cab pulled away from the street side. I turned, and flipping open my sketchbook, I glanced down at my apartment-hunting notes. I found the address, the notes scrolled next to it read:

shared one bedroom apt.
$2800 total rent
$1400 plus utilities

The brick was faded, but at least it wasn't crumbling like other places I had seen. I tried not to judge a book by its cover, but the bars on the windows did alarm me, and the scary man sitting on the stoop was not giving me the warm and fuzzies either. I took a deep breath and turned back to the street, arm stretched out to wave for a cab. Next.

CHAPTER 2

*L*ast night, when I called the number Paige had jotted down for me, it sounded like there had been a party going on in the background. She shouted the street address over the commotion, told me to be there at noon today, and hung up before I had a chance to ask any questions. I had no idea what I was walking into. She had called the place a loft, but I honestly didn't know what that meant. How many bedrooms were in a loft? How many roommates would I have? Were parties something I would have to deal with a lot?

I waffled back and forth all morning, debating if I should even keep the appointment. One thing was certain, classes were starting soon, and I was running out of time. I needed to get my housing situation figured out... and fast.

The previous night I had tried to do a search for the address she gave, to see if maybe Google Maps would reveal if the trip would be worth it. It only made me more nervous when it said the address could not be found. I heard a horn sound outside my motel window.

I thought staying at a motel on the outskirts of the city would be cheaper during the apartment hunt. What I hadn't considered was the cost of transportation. I had begun to dabble with the subway system, but still wasn't confident enough to use it on a regular basis.

Grabbing my favorite leather satchel, I tossed it over my shoulder. When I dressed myself this morning I took into consideration the look Paige had given me before, obviously regarding my bohemian style. Today I was much more confident in my attire. A white tank top, blue and white striped short sleeved sweater, and dark denim crop pants with oversized rolls at the calves, all complimented by a pair of white ballet flats. I was rather proud of the ensemble.

"Where to, miss?" the cabbie asked as I pulled the door closed.

"Corner of Fourteenth and Ninth, please," I answered, watching him for a reaction to the location. He gave me nothing, only pressed on the accelerator, and we were off.

When we arrived at the building I was certain something was off. I stared at the street side for a moment longer before repeating the address I had actually desired to the driver. He again confirmed this was the location. Settling the balance owed, I stepped out, watching the cab pull away. The street itself was actually quite quaint. There were trees lining both sides, and down a block I could see the start of some pristine looking row houses.

What I was staring at, however, was not quaint. It was a huge, oversized, dilapidated warehouse with a number of the windows boarded up. I glanced at the address I had jotted down: 16475. Looking to my left, and then right, I did my best to try and piece this puzzle together. That's when I spotted it. A door a few feet down on my left had the numbers 16475 spray painted above it. The paint was running, but the numbers were unmistakable.

My heart sank as I realized this was another dead end. There was no possible way this place could be livable. With a hard swallow, I decided to at least go in. I wasn't sure what was prompting me to keep this appointment. Perhaps it was because I had enjoyed talking to Paige. As sad as it was, Paige was the most contact I had with anyone in the city so far, except for my motel clerk who smelled like stale cigarettes and always stared at my breasts when he spoke to me.

Pulling the heavy metal door open, a blast of cool air and the smell of steel hit me. I walked inside to find an old lift—an actual lift, not an elevator—it was unlike anything I had ever ridden on before. I hesitated, unsure if I was even allowed to be in the place. Perhaps I had misread the numbers, and now I was trespassing. I pulled up the wooden gate and enclosed the cage around me. *Now what?* I wondered as I stared at the control board. One had a yellow star painted next to it so I decided to begin there.

Buzz.

The loud noise filled the car as I realized there was an intercom to the left of the control panel. My stomach twisted, nerves consuming me as the unfamiliar situation began to overwhelm me. I flexed my fingers, trying to calm myself.

23

Pressing the intercom button, I spoke, "I'm here to see Paige about an apartment."

Nobody replied. I stood there in awkward silence. A moment passed and the lift began to move. I sighed with relief; I had to be in the right place. The shaft moved slowly past the openings in the rickety wooden slat gate, until at last it came to a stop. Lifting the ancient gate, bits of white paint chipping off as I did, I stepped out onto a small landing with concrete floors, an oversized steel door in front of me. This door was actually quite beautiful with a patina all around the edges and a handsome sheen to it.

I reached out and knocked, the ting of steel against my knuckles filling the corridor.

"It's open," a man's voice called back.

A knot formed in my throat. That answered one question I had for Paige. Roommates? I couldn't see myself living with male roommates. Now I was certain this wasn't going to work out.

I pushed open the heavy door, stepping inside the vast space. The floors were no different than what had been in the corridor—unfinished concrete. I thought there was no way this could be a habitable dwelling, it had to be some sort of mistake.

"Hello?" I called out, feeling it was rude to walk too far into the space unescorted.

"Come on in," the faceless man called out from a hidden location.

Cautiously, I walked farther into the room, peering around the corner slowly. I was standing in the middle of a warehouse. It was exactly what it looked like from the outside, there was no mistaking it. It appeared as though a bunch of squatters had taken up residence in the space. A makeshift kitchen was off to one side, beaten down cabinets hung on the walls with no doors on the front of them, exposing the hodge-podge of cookware inside. The countertop was made of steel, and I would almost think it were stylish if it hadn't looked so filthy.

In the main room, the ceilings were open all the way to the rafters, and though there was a couch and some other random items of furniture strewn about, in no way did words like 'cozy' or 'home' come to mind. Off to one side was a hallway, which I had no desire to see what might reside on the other end.

"You've got to be kidding me," I mumbled, assuming I was alone in the room.

"About what?" the faceless voice called back. I quickly realized someone was lying on the couch.

"Oh, I'm sorry—I didn't see anyone. I'm here to see Paige," I replied.

"She's busy. I'm sure she'll be out soon," the raspy voice answered. I found myself getting annoyed at the fact this man continued to lay on the couch, out of sight, as I spoke to him. He obviously had no manners.

"I'm sorry, there must be some kind of mistake. Paige said this was a loft, and well, this is not what I pictured." I grimaced, confused by the picture before me. When I thought of a loft I imagined the glamorous images in magazines. This place definitely had the industrial thing going for it; after all, it was pretty much a factory floor with some furniture on it.

"And what exactly did you picture?"

"Something that didn't make me feel like I needed a tetanus shot after standing in it for ten minutes," I replied honestly.

With that, the faceless voice came into view. As he stood, my breath caught in my throat. He stared at me for a moment, not saying a word. I was fine with this because I found myself staring right back.

He stood there, just looking at me, one dark, sinister, and oh so sexy eyebrow raised. He was a shirtless Adonis, there in the flesh, and I was helpless, unable to look away. For a moment, my eyes shifted down, drinking in his firm chest, chiseled abs, and the tease of the cut just above where his distressed jeans rested. His muscles were hard, though his body still lean.

Quickly, when I realized I was ogling this stranger's body, I forced my eyes to shift back to his face, but there was no relief there from the exquisiteness. His straight, thick, dark black hair looked like he had just gotten out of bed, absolute perfection. I could even tell from the distance I stood, his eyes were a breathtaking icy gray. His complexion was flawless, accentuating the stubble of his three-day beard. He had a strong jawline that seemed to be clenched at the moment, and I couldn't help but wonder if he was annoyed by my presence.

"First off, no, this is not a loft. At least, not yet. It is a warehouse I'm in the process of converting to a loft space. Second, Paige doesn't live here." The words flew out of his mouth like spikes. I had obviously offended him. I turned my head, unable to carry on a conversation with him in his current state. The site of him, half-dressed, was actually starting to make me salivate.

26

"Wait, what?" I asked, seeking clarification, completely confused by this point, and embarrassed by my rudeness, but not willing to admit it.

"Oh, hey love!" Paige chirped strolling into the main room from the ominous dark hallway.

"Paige!" I exclaimed, relieved to see her face, though not much else about her seemed familiar. The hair, which had been blonde when I met her, was now auburn and wavy. Unable to help myself, I blurted out, "What happened to your hair?"

"Really? You didn't know that was a wig? I think the real question is what are you wearing? Are you going out on a yacht or something after this?" Paige asked with a snicker, continuing to grab a dirty bowl from the kitchen counter and rinse it. I heard the shirtless man also laugh, followed by the thud of him plopping back onto the couch. I was now glad I had not apologized for my rude comments.

I then noticed Paige's bare ass cheeks peeking out from under the oversized men's dress shirt she was wearing, the sliver of cotton at her waist barely qualifying as underwear. Suddenly, I felt something I had never felt in my life: old.

Deciding to ignore the nagging self-deprecating thoughts that were sneaking into my head, I chose to ignore her comment about my clothes and instead asked, "I thought you said you lived in a loft?"

"I do."

"This is not a loft!" I protested.

"I know. I don't live here," she replied, as if this were something I should have already known.

27

"Then why in the world would you tell me to meet you here?" I asked as Paige used the now only slightly soiled bowl to pour Cheerios into.

"She has a point. Quit telling people where I live!" the couch man called out from his hidden spot.

"Oh, shut up, Colin! It's your stupid fault I have to find a new roommate in the first place." Paige shouted through half chewed food.

Damn it, he looks like a Colin. *Stupid sexy people and their stupid sexy names*, I thought.

"What is going on out here?" a voice asked, walking out from the back room. He was wearing only boxer shorts, his body graced with muscles bulging from everywhere. His physique was very different from Colin's. He was bulky, his neck broad, and though they shared the same dark hair color, this one's was shorter, much more tailored.

The god-like creature walked up behind Paige, smacking her ass with one hand while wiping the sleep out of his eyes with the other.

"Oh nothing, just your brother being an ass," Paige snarled.

"You've got a real classy broad there, bro," Colin shot back.

"Can you two cool it for five minutes?" boxer boy asked, before looking around the kitchen with a puzzled stare, as if searching for something. "Hey babe, did you make me a bowl?"

Paige swallowed the bite in her mouth, and then replied, "You can use my bowl when I'm done."

I cringed at the complete lack of hygiene that

surrounded me. "Umm, hello? Remember me?"

"Oh, yeah, sorry. Clementine, this is my boyfriend, Christian. This place belongs to his brother—they're renovating it. I guess you've met Colin." After she finished speaking, she stuck her tongue at the invisible couch man.

Still stewing from his snickering in reference to Paige's joke about my clothes, I decided not to give him the satisfaction of my acknowledging his existence. "So, you don't live here?"

"No, I live in a loft a few doors down. I told you to meet me here because my roommate was getting her stuff out this morning, and I didn't want it to be all awkward."

"Why do you insist on calling your place a loft?" Colin asked, finally sitting up to make eye contact with someone he was engaged in a conversation with.

"Because it is," Paige growled, squinting at him from across the room.

"Oh my God, Paige, it's not! It is a two-bedroom apartment. There is nothing wrong with saying that. This place will be a loft."

"This place is a rat hole!" Paige shouted, her cheeks bright red.

"Fine, whatever, then why don't you go back to your own *loft*. And take Orange... Clementine... whatever her name is with you," Colin commanded.

If I hadn't been so insulted I was sure I could have come up with a witty response. "Nice to meet you, Christian. I'll wait for you outside, Paige," I instructed, turning and exiting. In the moment, I thought appreciating the introduction to his brother and not him would be quite a burn to Colin. Upon further reflection, I realized he probably didn't even notice.

* * *

CHAPTER 3

I took a step back, watching Paige as she fumbled with the keys in her hand, searching for the one that would provide access through the exterior security door. I wondered how she could look so fashionable in just a pair of cut off denim shorts and a button down shirt with a sheer scarf hanging around her neck. I could easily see her in the pages of a magazine, showing off the latest trends.

My first impression of the building was much better than of the warehouse space. The brick facade was well kept; below each window, flower boxes were perched, spilling over with color. At the edge of the street stood a tall oak tree in the small square of green space.

Paige sighed with relief after locating the correct key. Looking over her shoulder she explained, "I accidentally left my keys inside my place, so these are the spares I gave Christian, but he has all these blasted rental keys on his."

"Oh—" I began, following close behind her, "is he a handyman or something?"

Paige laughed at my question. "Not exactly. The Bennett brothers own around fifty properties. Well, I guess to be accurate, Colin owns them, but Christian helps with all the renovations and upkeep."

"Are they all as lovely as that last place?" I asked, horrific flashes of the warehouse running through my mind.

"Careful what you say about that place," Paige said, climbing a set of stairs in front of us. "That project is Colin's baby. He is sinking everything into it."

"Why? It's a wreck," I stated.

"Oh hell," Paige mumbled, halting at the top of the steps. I glanced around her to see a door propped open with a cardboard box.

"What's wrong?"

"Bitch is still here," Paige whispered looking back at me. I said nothing, unsure what she was talking about. "I guess we can still go in."

"Is everything all right?" I inquired, anxious about whatever situation seemed to be putting her on edge.

"My ex-roommate—she was supposed to be out by this morning, but she's still here." Paige took a deep breath, staring at the open door for a lingering moment.

"Things not end well?"

"It's complicated," Paige answered.

"Go ahead, tell her why it's complicated," an annoyed voice commanded from the doorway. Paige nearly jumped out of her skin.

"Bailey, hi, I didn't know you were going to be here. We'll just be in and out," Paige said, ignoring the girl's antagonizing remark.

"Whatever," the girl she had referred to as Bailey snarled, before huffing as she dropped another box in the hallway. The awkwardness of the encounter made my stomach flutter. The girl made no effort at hiding her complete and utter disgust at the situation she was in.

She was actually quite pretty: blonde, with perfectly sun kissed highlights. Her cheekbones were high, eyes a sparkling blue, and a figure that made me assume she must have been a model acquaintance. *Perhaps a working relationship soured?* I thought.

Turning sideways, I made my way past the angry girl, and followed Paige inside the door. The apartment immediately opened up to a galley kitchen, which would have seemed odd to me before, but after seeing so many apartments in New York, nothing surprised me any longer. The floors were a beautiful golden shade of oak hardwood, the cabinets a darker wood that almost appeared black at first glance, the countertop space was sparse, to say the least, but the swirling marble seemed to make up for the lack of space. The appliances were on the smaller side, but all stainless steel.

The kitchen led straight into a huge open living room that was flanked with two large oversized windows that overlooked that large tree by the street. The main wall to the left was exposed brick—a decorative fireplace place in the middle, with candles tucked into the opening. A gray sofa separated the room from the kitchen, a distressed coffee table in front of it, rested on top of an ornate teal and white rug. Between the windows sat a small side table with a lamp that was made out of what appeared to be driftwood, and to the right was an oversized cream linen chair. If you added a little art to the walls, it would instantly feel like home.

"It's a split bedroom layout. Your room has a bathroom with a stand up shower, but if I'm out you can use my bathroom, which has a tub," Paige explained.

"Are you serious?" I asked. The place seemed too good to be true. I was waiting for the catch.

"Serious about what?" Paige asked raising her eyebrows.

"This place seems too good. How much did you say rent would be?"

"For your half it's $1500, and that includes your utilities," Paige explained the terms. That was my entire monthly budget I was getting from school, which meant I would have to use savings and any money I could make to pay for food and other living expenses. I had naively hoped I would find a place for a fraction of my budget, but I was quickly learning this was not Indiana.

"Bailey, can I show her your old room?" Paige asked, attempting politeness.

"I don't give a crap, it's not mine anymore," the girl snapped, rushing past. Ever since we had entered the place, her packing efforts seemed to be in high gear.

"Slut," Paige whispered, walking toward the open bedroom to the right of the apartment. "This would be your bedroom. The bed and dresser stay, but you have to provide all of your own linens, and anything else you might need."

Paige stepped into the room, moving off to one side. The room was a unique shape with one of the exterior walls angling into the square footage. The same exterior wall was also exposed brick; the angled area had a window in the center of it. Behind Paige was the entrance to the modest bath. I couldn't help myself, I giggled.

"Is something funny?" she asked defensively.

"No, the place is great. I can't believe how many places I've looked at that didn't even have a window. What's the catch?"

I followed her as she walked back into the main living area. "No catch, just a good deal."

"Yeah, no catch, right," Bailey said sarcastically, walking past us to pick up another box.

"Grow up," Paige spat angrily.

The girl stopped in front of me, looking me up and down for a moment. "Word of advice, stay clear of the landlord."

"Umm, okay," I answered softly, shifting my weight from foot to foot uncomfortably.

"Shut up, Bailey, it was your choice to sleep with him. Why don't you quit blaming everyone else for your problems?" Paige pushed back, raising her voice.

"He cheated, Paige. He was wrong, not me," Bailey argued.

"Oh my God, I'm not doing this with you again!" Paige yelled, turning toward the door and walking out of the apartment, calling over her shoulder, "Leave your keys on the counter."

I stood there for a moment, staring at the girl whose anger had shifted to pain. I felt like I should say something, but I suddenly realized I was alone in the apartment with her. Without a word, I darted out into the hallway and down the steps, catching up with Paige on the sidewalk.

"What the hell was that?" I asked, a little unnerved by the confrontation.

"Want to get some coffee?" Paige asked, ignoring my question.

"I suppose," I answered, secretly eager to wrap up the deal.

"There's a great place down a block, Ninth Street Espresso. They make an insanely good espresso with milk." Paige was clearly focused on not talking about what had just happened.

"Never had one," I replied.

"Never had what?" Paige asked, shoving her hands into her pockets, wiggling a stray pebble loose from her gladiator sandals.

"An espresso," I answered flatly.

"Like, ever?" she asked.

"I tend to just drink plain old black coffee," I explained. "I guess I'm boring that way."

"You've got to learn to live a little my friend," Paige commanded, flashing me a brief smile.

"So I have to tell you, I love the apartment, if you're interested in having me move in, I would really like to rent the room from you for the next two semesters." I held my breath, hoping she was as interested in me as I was in the unit.

Paige stopped just outside the door of a shop with a coffee cup decal on the glass. She looked at me through squinted eyes. "You're not going to end up going all single white female on me like Bailey, are you?"

"Well, since I don't know how she went all crazy on you I can't make any promises," I replied, in hopes I might get more of the mysterious ex-roommate picture.

"Fair enough," Paige said with a shrug, not taking the bait, and opened the door.

When I walked into the narrow shop I was in awe. Everything in the city still seemed to wow me. Where I came from, we had either Starbucks or the country diners. There was nothing like these trendy coffee shops. Behind the counter was a map of the world splayed across the back wall, and in the corner the words, 'Ninth Street Espresso' were stenciled. A simple sign hung at one end of the counter with the minimalist menu displayed across it, making your choice simple. However, Paige was right; I wanted to live a little. I wanted to try everything. Paige made the decision easy for me when she ordered two espressos and milk.

I pulled my money from my pocket, preparing to pay, when she waved me off with a smile. "Hey Bill," she chirped to the man at the register, moving down to wait for her order. They made small talk for a moment, and I wondered how often she came to the location. Once the order was ready she snatched up the cups and turned to take a seat. I lifted my eyebrows, clearly puzzled by the transaction not involving the exchange of money.

Paige giggled and then whispered, "The boys own this building. They haven't made me pay for coffee since I started dating Christian."

"Wow, nice perk," I replied, taking a seat across from her. She slid the small cup in front of me, and I watched the steam rise off of it, dancing through the air.

Raising her cup, she extended her hand in my direction, gesturing a toast. As the cups clanged together she said, "To trying new things."

I could tell Paige liked to try new things. It was obvious she was not afraid to live; even when she walked it seemed like her small frame translated to a beast on the prowl, searching for an adventure. I envied that about her. I missed my four walls in Indiana, the security, and the sanctuary of solitude it had become for me. It wasn't who I had wanted to become, but simply who I was comfortable being.

"So—" I pushed, "are you going to tell me the story about your ex-roomy, or do I just have to guess?"

"Your guessing might be fun," Paige answered with a grin.

I sipped the drink, the creamy dream of it lingering on my tongue. The bitterness, and reason I had never tried one, were nowhere to be found. Another thing I had been missing out on because of my baseless fears. "Oh my God! This is so good."

"Stick with me, hon, there are so many good things I can show you in this city." I couldn't decide if her offer excited or frightened me, but then I decided it was perhaps a little of both.

"So back to crazy girl story," I said with a laugh.

"There's not much to tell. She slept with Colin and tried to make it into something more than it was. Totally became a stalker chick," Paige's voice carried an intense disdain.

"Wait, what?" I gasped. "Colin is your landlord?"

"Yeah? Why do you think I get such a good deal?

Christian and I have been together since we were kids," Paige explained.

"Does the guy own the entire block? This is insane." I thought of the way he looked, trying to figure out exactly how old he was, but all I could remember was his flat stomach and that he had called me Orange.

"It's complicated. A lot of messed up shit happened to the boys pretty early. Colin has always been driven. Say what you will about him, but he never beats around the bush when it comes to women he sees. I know it seems like I argue with him, but it's more like a big bro, little sis thing with us. He wasn't even interested in Bailey; she was the one who kept pushing it. He let her know it was a one time thing, but she thought she could make it into more."

"So, he's a player?" I asked, not shielding my revolt. I wasn't surprised that someone as hot as him had such little respect for women.

Paige laughed. "I don't know. I guess. I don't think of him that way. He just doesn't want commitment right now, you know?"

"I guess." I did know. Perhaps not in the same way as Colin, but the last thing I wanted again was a relationship. After Ashton I made up my mind it was best for all parties involved that I stay away from love.

"Colin isn't all bad. Just don't sleep with him, and you won't have a problem," Paige instructed.

"No problem there, I'm completely uninterested."

"Really? Not your type? Or do you already have a boyfriend?" Paige inquired, leaning forward, eager to get the scoop on my life.

"He isn't even remotely my type." Because no man was

my type. "I had a relationship end badly, I'm just looking to get through this last year of school."

"Oh school—that's right. You need a space to paint. Do you want me to ask Colin if you can use part of the warehouse to paint? I know there's a lot of vacant space in there right now. He'd probably even let you use it free of charge since you're my roommate now," Paige offered.

"No!" I quickly replied. I wanted nothing from the king of one-night stands. The idea of even living in an apartment he owned kind of made my skin crawl. "I can work at our apartment, or there's studio space at school I can reserve."

"All right," Paige said, flopping back into her chair and shrugging. "Just an idea."

"Thanks, I appreciate it," I said, pushing my lips together into a half-hearted smile.

"When did you plan to move in?" Paige asked looking out the large glass window, watching the people walking by on the street.

"I don't have much stuff, it's all back at the motel. If it's all right, I can go get it now and be moved in tonight," I offered, hoping the aggressive move in schedule wouldn't be a problem.

"Awesome!" Paige said. "And actually, Bailey was paid up through the end of the month so don't worry about paying until September first."

"Are you sure?" I asked, shocked by her generosity.

"Yeah, it's not a problem. I guess I can call you Emmie now." Paige gave me a grin, a red curl hanging over one eye. I remembered the cab ride and the comment she had made about us being strangers. There was that wit again.

* * *

CHAPTER 4

I pulled the phone away from my ear for a moment as I slipped my shirt over my head. "Yes, Mom, I'm sure everything will be fine."

"I mean it, Emmie, you don't know these people. How do you know this Paige girl isn't into drugs or something worse?" my mother's soft voice queried.

"Seriously? Did you just ask me that?" I chuckled, throwing my bag, which was heavily weighted with fresh art supplies, over my shoulder, and rushing out the door. Pulling it shut as I left, I dropped my keys into the pocket of the shirt Paige had let me borrow. She apparently felt my wardrobe was unfit for such a momentous occasion as the first day of classes. I had to leave it unbuttoned to account for the fact that my breasts were at least three times larger than hers. She offered to let me wear one of her tanks that had a slit down the middle of the chest, but I assured her my undershirt would suffice.

"I am absolutely serious. When I told you to go to New

York I never imagined you would have to live with a complete stranger," Mom rebutted.

As I turned the corner, beginning my seven-block march to school, I rolled my eyes. She had been the one to practically push me out the door when I left Indiana, and now she was freaking out on me. "What did you think would happen? Do you actually know how expensive New York is?"

"I don't know, I figured there would be some kind of dorm or something." I knew she was worried, and I was pretty sure she was missing me as much as I was missing her.

"Well, that's not how it works, but don't worry, please. Paige is very sweet, and her boyfriend only lives a couple doors down so if anything goes wrong I am sure he will be there in heartbeat," I said, attempting to comfort her.

"What kind of thing would go wrong?" she pushed, now sounding even more panicked.

"Oh my God, Mom! Really? Nothing is going to go wrong, I am just trying to make you feel better," I admitted. I tapped my foot impatiently at the corner light, waiting for the walk sign.

"Well, what about this other character you were telling me about? Her boyfriend's brother or something?" Leave it to my mom to fish out any information where a man was involved.

"Colin?" I asked, already knowing exactly whom she was talking about.

"Yeah. Is he okay?"

"I'm not sure what you mean by okay, but since I don't live with him, and have no intentions of speaking much to him, I don't think you have anything to worry about." My tone was clearly sounding agitated. "Look Mom, I'm almost to school. I need to call you back, all right?"

I crossed the street quickly, practically being carried by the sea of people around me. "I worry, Emmie. Sorry if that upsets you."

"I'm not upset, Mom, I just really have to go," I explained, before saying goodbye and attempting to end the call. Instead of ending the call, however, the phone flipped out of my hand. In an attempt to catch the device, I outstretched my arm, causing the weight of my bag to pull me forward and send me toppling over, my belongings spilling out and the contents sliding across the sidewalk, landing near my phone.

"Shit!" I exclaimed, pulling the strap from over my head and scooping the randomly strewn items into my bag. I wasn't one who would normally curse, but it seemed as though the moment merited the frustration.

Reaching out for the culprit of the disaster, my phone, my hand instead met with the back of someone else's hand. Following with my fingertips, I made my way up to a strong and muscular arm, realizing someone else had beat me to the phone.

Startled, I hopped to my feet not noticing the man had extended his other hand to me in assistance. When I was again upright my eyes shifted around wildly, mostly staring at the hand that had my phone concealed within it. I wasn't sure why, but the entire situation made me anxious, that is, until he reached out with his empty hand and touched my arm.

"Are you all right?" he asked, staring at me as if he were inspecting me for damages.

"Umm—" *Really? Umm, is all you can come up with?* I internally scolded myself.

Instead of delivering an intelligent line, I stared blankly. The man was gorgeous in a rugged and mischievous way. His eyes were dark, his stubble just beginning to show, his jawline wide and strong, a dimple on one cheek. He kept his chestnut hair trimmed tight on the sides, but the top slightly messed. I'm not sure what came over me in that moment, but I lifted a single hand and fell forward, using his firm chest to catch myself.

What was I doing? I had now succumbed to groping a complete stranger.

"You seem lightheaded, come sit," he followed up, taking my arm and leading me to a nearby stone column, the perfect height for sitting.

Yeah, lightheaded! I thought. I decided I'd run with that. "I'm so sorry, I don't know what's wrong with me—"

"Stryker," the man said, as if spewing some sort of cryptic code at me.

"Pardon me?" I asked.

"My name... it's Stryker. William Stryker, but all my friends call me Stryker."

I'm not sure what possessed me to say the next thing that came out of my mouth. I blame Paige. Somehow, in a short amount of time she had managed to corrupt me. "Well, since we're strangers what should I call you?" In my mind I kept thinking Mr. Sexy Pants seemed appropriate.

"What?" he asked, a puzzled look on his face.

I couldn't even deliver the line correctly. "I just meant

—since I don't know you, we're not friends, and therefore I can't call you Stryker, what should I call you instead?"

Yup, I had actually managed to make it worse.

"Well, how about you call me Stryker, too?"

"Sounds good," I replied, giving up on being clever.

"What's your name?" he asked, handing me my phone.

"Clementine," I answered, smiling. He didn't react the way people normally did to my name. I usually got an, 'Oh, isn't that unique.' The best, of course, were the ones who joked, 'Didn't your mom love you?' Instead he just nodded.

"Well, I hope to see you around, Clementine," he added, turning and walking toward the entrance to the school.

"Thanks," I called out after him, like a complete dork. What had gotten into me? It was like I had never seen a hot guy before. Apparently all of the guys in New York were hotties, but that was beside the point. I wasn't interested in men, even if they did make me lose temporary control of my senses. I was there to get my degree and that's it—nothing else. Certainly nothing that would involve sexy men.

CHAPTER 5

I did it! I made it through my first day of classes and the earth did not spin off its axis, no natural disasters of any kind seemed to be occurring. Perhaps I was going to make it through this next year without falling apart, after all. The walk back to the apartment had been one of the most amazing walks of my life, although nothing special happened exactly. The wind was blowing through my hair, the car horns still blared, but I didn't seem to notice them anymore. The hair on my arms was standing up, and I could feel my heart fluttering. I think it was happiness, or maybe contentment. It had been so long since I felt either.

In my very first class, the moment the professor had us take out our pads and pencil for still-life studies, I melted into a giddy mess. I could hear most of the students groaning as they dug through their bags, clearly not excited by the random objects set up around the room for us to draw. For me, it was different. I was coming from a place none of them could understand. This was something I had always wanted, and at last, I was not going to let my tragedy define me. I was doing this for me.

Shoving the key into the security door, I turned the lock, making my way inside. I was probably the only student excited by the fact we had homework on the first day of class. I couldn't imagine how any other artist could look at what we did as work. When I sketched or painted, it felt like breathing. Lugging my oversized bag up the stairs, I gladly dropped it in the hall as I unlocked the apartment. *My New York apartment*: the mere thought of it made me want to squeal in delight.

As I pushed open the door, using my hip, I could hear muffled sounds coming from the living room. Bending over, I picked up my belongings and without raising my head, stepped inside. I allowed the door to close behind me. Paige and I had not discussed our schedules yet, but I was getting the distinct impression she didn't really have a set schedule. Plopping the keys down on the kitchen counter, I made my way into the living room and prepared to set my bag onto the couch.

Much to my surprise, as I came into the room, I realized the couch was, in fact, occupied. A man's sculpted, bare ass was staring up at me.

"Oh my God!" I blurted out, unable to move.

Propping himself up with one arm, he shifted his weight to reveal Paige beneath him. She sat up, not bothering to cover her small breasts from my sight. "Umm, hello. Yeah sorry about this, I didn't think you'd be back for a while."

For the life of me, I couldn't think of a single thing to say; instead, I used all of my energy to close my jaw, which I realized had been hanging open for some time. Raising my hand to cover my eyes, I turned toward the door from which I had just entered, grabbed my keys, and made my quick exit, bag still over my shoulder.

There was no way I just saw that... was there? I couldn't get the image of Christian's naked body out of my mind. At least he didn't stand up. I was certain that would be something I could never shake. Bursting from the front door of the building I began to pace back and forth in front of the apartment. I had lived with this girl for one day and had already managed to see her and her boyfriend completely naked. They did not, however, seem to find this as distressing.

I suddenly realized I had another predicament—did they stop after I left, or had they simply continued their activities? There was no way I could return to the scene of the crime, so I would need to find somewhere to sketch for a few hours before returning. They would certainly have to be done by then. The coffee shop Paige had taken me to would have to serve as a temporary studio, and with a huff I began the walk in that direction, contemplating the talk I needed to have with Paige later that evening.

"Em?" I recognized Colin's voice immediately. Of course I would run into him right now, after just witnessing his brother having a naked romp with my new roommate. And Em? Where did he get off calling me Em?

"Hi," I offered politely as I walked past, careful not to commit myself to an actual conversation.

"Hey, wait up, I was just coming to talk to you," he

added, grabbing hold of my elbow, causing me to grind to a halt outside of his building.

I looked down at the placement of his hand on my arm. I couldn't decide if I was revolted or enjoyed the warm touch.

"I'm sorry, I didn't mean to grab you," he said, witnessing my internal dilemma.

"No, it's fine," I answered, turning to face him. "You were coming to see me? Why on earth—"

"Paige told me you were going to be her new room-mate," Colin began. His dark hair plastered itself against his forehead in the blustery wind. I found myself staring as his gray eyes shimmered.

"Oh right, of course," I said, the situation becoming clear to me. "You're my new landlord. Paige said I would just pay her every month, and she took care of everything with you. Is that not right?"

"No, that's not why I wanted to talk to you," he contin-ued. I froze, staring at him through confused eyes. I couldn't imagine any other reason he might possibly want to see me. We had made it more than clear to one another, upon meeting, that we detested the other's company.

"Oh?" I decided it best to keep my answers short.

"Were you headed out?" he asked, noticing my direction.

"Well—" I hesitated, unsure how to explain my current predicament. "Actually, I just got home, but the apartment seems to be otherwise occupied."

"Paige and Christian," Colin laughed. "Yeah, my brother can be a bit of a tasteless dick sometimes."

"Yeah, your brother," I muttered under my breath,

thinking about the poor ex-roommate of Paige's I had recently met. I was confident he had learned most of his inappropriate behavior from his big brother.

"What?" he asked, as I quickly regretted my snarky response. It was one thing to think he was a womanizing prick, but something quite different to actually have a discussion with him about these thoughts.

"Oh, nothing," I replied.

Colin furrowed his eyebrows, one swooping lower than the other, and I wondered how in the hell he could look so damn sexy, even with a scowl on his face. It was infuriating he could look so good all of the time. "Okay, whatever. I used to have a problem with them not respecting my place with their extracurricular activities, but after a quick talk with Christian, it hasn't been a problem since. I'm sure if you tell Paige, she'll rein it in."

"I'll try that. Is that all?" I asked, eager to break away from his mesmerizing gaze.

"No, are you in a hurry or something?" Colin asked, starting to sound slightly irritated with me.

"I just have a lot of work to do. I was headed to a coffee shop to get started," I partially explained.

"You should try Ninth Street Espresso sometime. It's great."

Of course he would recommend the coffee shop that was in the building he owned. Not that I would give him the satisfaction of knowing that was where I was going anyway.

"So, was there was something else?" I pushed, glancing over my shoulder so he would know I was ready to be on my way.

"You know, everyone in this city works out of coffee shops, right? You'll be lucky to even get a table this time of day. Why not come in and work here? I have plenty of space for you to spread out. I'll even make you a cup of coffee. I don't have my espresso machine hooked up yet, but I can make a mean cup from the French press," Colin offered.

On one hand, I loathed him for the fact that he had an espresso machine of his own, and on the other, I wanted to hug him because I found a fellow French presser. Though he had a point about being able to work comfortably, I didn't really want to go into his home and have an ongoing conversation with the creep. "I don't know."

"Oh, come on, I'd be insulted if you didn't. It's the least I can do after my brother put you out like this."

He did have a point about that. I didn't care if he was insulted or not, and the fact that he thought I would care only reminded me more why I disliked him.

"I really have a lot to do… I shouldn't," I reiterated.

"I promise, I'll only talk to you while I make the coffee, and then I'll be as quiet as a mouse. I have a tiling job in the bathroom to get done, so I doubt you will even see me." I couldn't figure out why he wanted me to come in so badly. Only a day ago he had snarled at me to get out of his place and mockingly referred to me as Orange. However, I was eager to start on my assignments, and a quiet place to work would be nice.

"All right," I relented.

"Great, come on in," Colin said, holding the door open for me. We were both silent until we made it into the apartment. I didn't dare look at him, but I could feel his eyes on me, studying me. I wondered if he realized I was wearing one of Paige's shirts.

"Will the living room work?" he asked as he made his way into the kitchen, immediately pulling out the small red press.

Though the accommodations had seemed quite unfitting to live in, as a workspace, the warehouse was ideal. "Yes, thank you," I answered.

"You can help yourself to anything you need. I'll be working in the master bath, but there is also a bathroom down that hall if you need one."

Placing my bag on the couch, I looked around the place, a little in awe that he didn't find such a huge project overwhelming. Attempting to ease the awkwardness, I made my effort at small talk, careful not to seem too friendly. "This looks like a big undertaking."

"Yeah, it is. The biggest project I've ever taken on. I can't decide from one day to the next if I want to jump for joy or throw up." Colin laughed as he poured the coffee grounds into the device. Had I not had a little of his history told to me beforehand, I might have actually fallen for his charms.

I wanted to ask why he was talking to me? Why would I care about how nervous his next rich boy venture made him? Why would I care anything about him? I wanted to tell him how disgusting he was for treating women like they were objects, to be played with and then discarded. But I didn't ask those things; I simply nodded with a half-smile, arranging my supplies carefully on the reclaimed wood coffee table.

"Well, good luck," I lied. I didn't wish anything bad to

happen to the man, but I also couldn't care less if anything good happened to him.

"Thanks," he called across the room, placing the filled kettle onto the stove top before making his way over to my location. "Clementine, I—"

"Emmie, you can call me Emmie," I interrupted. I actually did not consider him a friend, but when he called me Clementine it only reminded me of his Orange comment. At least if he was calling me Emmie I didn't want to strangle him—mostly.

"All right." He seemed very pleased with the nickname offer. "Emmie. I wanted to talk to you because of my behavior when we met."

"Excuse me?" I asked, unsure if I was actually hearing him correctly.

"I know I can be a bit sensitive about this project. You have to understand, I have a lot riding on this, so when a beautiful stranger came in and was so honest about the current condition of this place, it kicked my defense into overdrive. I was rude to you, and for that, I'm sorry."

My mouth dropped open. Did he really just have the nerve to call me beautiful? Was he flirting with me? Was that a bad thing? Wait, girl, listen to yourself. Of course it was a bad thing. He chewed women up and spit them out. Besides, you didn't come here for love! Focus! Don't look at his eyes, don't look, no, don't do it. Damn it! I looked. How did he do that? It was almost like he smiled with those gray pools of intensity. Oh God, when did I get so cheesy?

"It's fine," I replied, pleased I had avoided coming unraveled on the exterior.

"So, you're an artist? Do you have anything you can show me?" he asked, and I was sure he was only pretending to be interested.

Before I could say anything, the kettle began to rock, the water within boiling. He turned back and rushed over to relieve it from the heat, transferring the liquid quickly to the press.

I stared as he waited for the perfect timing. "Nothing here, really. I sell my work online, so you could go there and see a lot of my stuff."

"Oh wow, you're already selling your work, huh?"

I couldn't help myself—talking about my art was something I was proud of—even if he was a pig, it didn't change the fact that I still loved my craft. "I've actually been selling my stuff for a couple years. I've had over three thousand paintings and prints sell."

"Holy crap, that's amazing. Why bother with college? Sound like you're doing great on your own. I never bothered with college myself, seemed like a waste of money."

Of course he skipped college, his parents probably started buying him properties as soon as he could walk. I had been around enough wealthy people in my life. Ashton was the same way—he never had a clue about how real people in the world made it. I think that was why he always struggled once his dad's business went under.

"I want to be better at what I do," I offered, my answer completely sincere.

"Sounds to me like there are a lot of people who think you do what you do just fine." Colin suggested, pouring the black richness into two mismatched mugs.

I didn't respond. I couldn't. He was right, I had already

achieved a lot of success in my art career. I wasn't about to explain my past to him—that I had wanted to go to art school since high school, and I lost that dream because I married a bully. A guy that probably respected women about as much as he did. Then, when I decided I would go and achieve that dream, that bully took everything I had left away from me. I needed this, I needed school to help me find my way back to what I wanted before I became Ashton's widow. Nobody got to know that part of who I was, though; that belonged to me.

"You can always be better," I finally said.

"I suppose. Cream or sugar?" he asked searching around for the items he had offered me.

"Black." When I replied, he looked relieved, then placed the mug carefully on table near me.

"Careful, it's hot," he warned, turning back to retrieve his mug. "Well, Emmie, you're welcome to work here whenever you need a break from Paige and my brother's incessant savagery. If my work is too loud, there is plenty of space in this building, so we can find a spot for you."

I wondered if Paige had said something to him about studio space, despite my protests. "Thanks, I'll keep that in mind."

"I won't model nude for you, though, so don't ask. All right, maybe if you say please," Colin said, turning to deliver a wicked grin. Leaning back against the counter and raising the mug to his lips, he watched, waiting for me to come undone by his comment.

There it was, that egocentric, degenerate, smug attitude I knew was lurking just below the surface. "Don't worry, I won't."

My reaction was clearly not what he expected. I pulled out my sketchpad and flipped it open to the shading exercise we had been given. Plopping down on the couch, with my back to Colin, I was confident I had sent him the message I intended, loud and clear.

"So, is there a boyfriend back home in—where are you from again?" He clearly had not gotten the message.

Glancing over my shoulder, I replied as coolly as possible without being rude, "Indiana, and no, I'm not interested in dating right now. I have a lot of work to do, so was there anything else?"

I was quite proud of the way I was asserting myself with him. It had always been something I had failed at in my younger years. It didn't take much pushing for people to get me to do what they wanted. I had no intention of repeating those same mistakes.

"No, sorry, I'll let you get to it then." His smirk faded, eyelids dropping to where I could no longer see his irises. His disappointment was obvious. For a brief moment I wavered, considering an apology for my rude behavior, but then decided to hold strong as he exited the room.

I could hear the occasional clinking of tiles, but I did not see him again that night. After a couple hours passed, I assumed it was safe to return home to the apartment, and snuck out. I knew it was rude to leave without a word, but I couldn't fathom what to possibly say to him.

CHAPTER 6

*T*he first week of school was over, and I had somehow managed to avoid Colin for the remainder of it. I didn't even need to take his advice about talking to Paige about her and Christian's activities. When I got home that first day, she was waiting for me on the couch. After apologizing profusely, she assured me they would keep their alone time confined to her bedroom.

Though I was appreciative of the sentiment, I still wasn't sure how soon I would be sitting on that couch. Of course, based on their boldness with such activities, I wasn't sure if many spots in the apartment would be untainted.

I worked on my sketches in my bedroom and used the school studio for my paintings. It was working out exactly like I had envisioned it. Occasionally the space was booked, but nothing I couldn't work around. I was focusing on my work and successfully avoiding distractions. Now here I was, my first Saturday as an actual New York resident, and I was eager to experience everything. I had gotten up early and visited the farmer's market in Chelsea.

After a quick trip home to unload my bags of goodies, I packed up my travel portfolio, excited for an afternoon of sketching in the park. I wasn't sure if all the members of this amazing city appreciated what they had at their fingertips all of the time, but it was clear some did.

People were out in droves, enjoying the outdoor time with their pets and loved ones. When I used to see couples, huddled close together, it would bother me, but now I could actually look around and not burst into uncontrolled sobbing fits. That was probably one of the hardest feelings to wrestle with: I was leaving Ashton, yes, but to have him completely taken away from me—someone I loved no longer be part of the world I was walking around in—created an unexplainable emptiness.

Arriving at the 14th Street Park, I was pleased to find an area with grass, but also amazed at what little green space qualified as a park in this city. Opening the gate that surrounded the place, I struggled to balance the lunch I had packed, a blanket, and my art supplies as they over-flowed in my arms. As I attempted to close the gate behind me to ensure no animals or children could slip out unnoticed, my sketchpad fell from my grasp, hitting the sidewalk and sending the loose pages scattering in the wind.

"Crap!" I exclaimed, dropping the remainder of my items and giving chase to the random sheets, blowing about. Stretching out one arm and a leg, I extended my toe as far as I could stretch it in order to press a sheet against the ground, engaging in the invisible game of solo twister. As quickly as possible, I gathered up the drawings, my cheeks burning from the sheer embarrassment of my clumsiness.

Frantically, I shoved the pages into the back of my sketchbook, looking around to ensure I hadn't missed one. Confident I had them all I made my back to the gate where a man was standing, giving me a disapproving look for leaving it ajar, unaware of the efforts I had made to avoid that. Based on the tiny Chihuahua in his arms, his beloved companion had attempted an escape.

"I'm sorry, my arms were full, and I was trying to balance it all, but then my stuff fell, and the wind, well—it was a mess. Sorry." I realized quickly my speedy apology sounded more like rambling. After the man with the ascot decided he had gotten his point across with his snotty look, he turned to head back into the park and engage in more play time with his tiny sidekick, who, based on the incessant barking, seemed to dislike me as much as his owner.

Using my foot to kick the rest of my belongings into the park I secured the gate behind me before scooping up my bag and blanket. The beautiful shady areas, underneath the few trees, were all taken, and I was left spreading out my blanket in an open area, the blazing sun directly overhead. I was determined not to let the start of this excursion deter me, certain I would have a good time if I simply resolved myself to the fact I would.

I sat my sketchpad down and placed my packed lunch on top to guarantee I didn't have a repeat of the great tornado of art incident. I spread out my blanket, folding it in half so I wouldn't take up more space than a single person should. On my knees, organizing my remaining belongings around myself—sweat was already causing my sunglasses to shift down my nose.

I flipped open my pad and searched the pockets in my oversized patchwork hooded vest for my pencil. I tidied up the pages before staring at the blankness before me. One of my professors instructed we go out and sketch things in motion, pulling things from real life to see what art comes of them. Across the park I saw the man with the ascot playing with his dog... no definitely not.

On the opposite side of the park was a young couple openly sharing their expression of love on a park bench with some public groping... nope, not going to work. A small child was playing near her parents who were arguing in the background... nope, too depressing.

"Is this yours?" an oddly familiar male voice asked from behind me.

I turned, surprised to see Mr. Sexy Pants, whom I had met a week ago, staring at me, holding a sketch of a fruit bowl. Apparently I had not found all the victims of the art tornado.

"Hey, it's you! Clementine, right?" Oh my God, he remembered my name. What was his name? The only thing I could think of was Mr. Sexy Pants. Damn it!

"Yeah, hi!" I exclaimed making it clear I did in fact recognize him. What was his name?

"So—is this yours?" he asked extending a hand with my work.

"Yes, thank you so much. I had a little mishap when I got here, and the wind must have carried it away."

"Well, you don't want to lose such a masterpiece."

Damn it, he was hot *and* nice. Just ask him. "I'm sorry, I'm afraid I can't remember your name."

"Really?" he asked and then laughed.

"Is that funny?" I was confused by his reaction.

"Kind of, since I have a name people tend not to forget. I was teased a lot growing up, and I'm just surprised you could forget it." First, I had trouble believing anyone could make fun of him, and second, I felt even worse I had forgotten his name now.

"I'm sorry."

"Oh, it's no problem. William Stryker." That was it! Now I remembered. He motioned toward the blanket, clearly wanting to take a seat. "May I?"

I hesitated. I had no idea who this man was and wasn't sure if I felt comfortable cozying up to a perfect stranger.

"Unless you're already waiting for someone else, of course," he added, sensing my edginess.

"No, of course not, have a seat," I replied. *Calm down. It's no big deal, he's just a nice guy and you're only having a conversation with him. Stop being such a spaz,* I told myself.

"Didn't you say you were working for the school? Are you a professor or something?" I made a feeble attempt at small talk.

"No, no—" he began, shaking his head. "Nothing like that. I'm doing some consulting work."

"Oh really? What kind of consulting work does a school need?" I questioned, truly interested in what he had to say.

He didn't answer right away, and looking around the park, I wondered if perhaps his work was sensitive in some way. Then looking back at me, he explained, "Some-times they hire people, and before they give out certain positions they want to make sure that they are hiring someone who won't have—oh, how do I say this gently, any skeletons in their closets."

"You're a cop? No way!" I cried out in disbelief.

"Oh hell no, nothing like that. Let's just say, I'm really good at research. What about you? Are you a freshman?" he asked.

It was obvious I wasn't an eighteen year old girl anymore, so for him to ask if I were a freshman, I was certain he was trying to flatter me. The compliment unnerved me and exhilarated me at the same time. It had been so long since a man noticed me, and even though I wasn't seeking it, the bigger problem was I didn't know how to react to the attention.

"Nice one," I laughed.

"What? I'm serious? Are you a student there?"

"Yeah, I'm a transfer student. I'm finishing up my studios there so I can graduate," I explained, surprised by how good it made me feel to say those words.

"Based on what I've seen, you're very talented." He was laying it on thick, never shifting his eyes from me. I had always been self conscious of the way my face was so round. It never seemed to matter if I thinned out... my face was always thick. My mom used to call it baby fat, which only made it worse. He didn't seem to notice, his gaze never shifting from my blue eyes no matter how much I avoided looking at his.

"That's very kind of you to say, thank you, and also very hard to determine from a sketch of a fruit bowl."

"It's the best damn fruit bowl I've ever seen," he said, leaning forward and flashing his broad white smile.

"I'm already beginning to see that I'm behind other students. I think doing my courses through correspondence made it harder on me. I just don't have the same hands on and critiquing experience some of the other students have had."

"You can't tell," he insisted, reaching over and lifting a couple pages into my sketchbook, revealing the hidden images. "These really are fantastic. What were you working on before I so rudely interrupted?"

"You weren't rude." I giggled as I replied, and I wondered who the hell had taken over my body. "After all, you rescued my fruit bowl."

"That I did. But you didn't answer me. What were you working on?" He rested himself on one arm, lying on his side with his legs crossed as he stared up at me. I watched as he licked his lips, and I struggled to think of what to say next.

"Nothing!" I shouted, excited to remember any word in the English language. He smiled at me; he must have thought I was a mad woman. "I mean, I hadn't decided what to draw yet. We're supposed to pick something in motion that we find in real life."

"Hmm..." he hummed, sitting up, brows furrowed, clearly deep in thought about my assignment.

"What?" I probed, truly curious about the idea he obviously consumed by.

"How about this?" Stryker asked, hopping to his feet. He proceeded to extend his arms outward. One fingertip jerked, and he proceeded to perform an arm wave that rippled through his body.

I burst out laughing, looking all around us to see who

64

was watching. There were a few onlookers, but Stryker didn't seem to care. He didn't take his eyes off me. He just continued staring at me, wiggling his body around wildly for me.

"That's perfect!" I squealed, quickly placing pencil to paper and capturing the fluid movement.

"What I won't do for art. But you have to credit me as your muse," he added, laughing.

I don't know why I let him sit, and I certainly don't know why I ended up drawing fifteen sketches of him that day. He was handsome, that was for certain. I knew I didn't want to start dating anyone. Love was not in the plans for this phase of my life.

I also don't know why I said yes when he asked me if I wanted to have dinner, but I did. After he left me there, in the park, I realized I had been smiling so long my face was hurting. But the fact that I didn't know why I said yes to all of these things didn't change the fact that I had agreed to have dinner with him that very night. He would be picking me up at the apartment in a matter of hours.

CHAPTER 7

hat the hell are you doing, girl? I stared in the mirror, repeatedly asking myself that question. Thanks to a lot of hair product, I had managed to tame my frizzy, dirty blonde mess into oversized, gentle curls. Leaning forward I checked for any stray, unruly eyebrow hairs that might need plucked. One last touch up of blush and an additional layer of mascara should be enough. As I applied the makeup the thought rushes through my head again: *What the hell are you doing?*

When I left Indiana I swore to myself I wouldn't lose focus. I was determined I would keep my head down, make it through the year, and get my ass back home. I was here to experience things, as long as it didn't include men. Countless museums and parks were on my list of must-sees. Dating was for certain on my list of don'ts. Ashton had been my first real boyfriend, my first kiss, my first everything. A first love that ends in such tragedy can only mean one thing: I was not cut out for love. Yet, here I was.

I made the mistake of telling Paige I had a date, and

since that moment she was like a dog with a bone. She wanted to know everything about him, although I didn't have much to tell her—only what we had discussed that day in the park. It didn't take long for her attention to shift to my evening's wardrobe choice. She was less than impressed by the sundress I had chosen. Instead, she pulled a little black number out of her closet for me.

I was certain my size ten curves were not going to fit into anything she had in her size two closet, but leave it to Paige—she found the one dress I could squeeze into. The black spandex gave in all the places it needed to in order to fit my frame. I wasn't as convinced as Paige when I put it on. I believe her exact words were 'smoking hot.' All I could see when I looked in the mirror was cleavage and a bubble butt. After Paige left to meet Christian I seriously considered changing back into my own clothes. A part of me resisted; I should really find that part and strangle it.

I walked out of my bathroom and into my small, but well organized bedroom, slipping on the one pair of heels I had brought with me from Indiana: a simple and plain pair of matte black stilettos. High heels were something I considered having a love/hate relationship with. They made my long legs look amazing, lengthening my calves and making them appear athletic. They also made my feet ache, and I usually had a two-hour time limit on actually wearing them. However, they were the only shoes that did the dress Paige lent me justice.

Lipstick and I'm ready. My mother had taught me when I was just a girl to always apply lipstick last to keep it looking fresh as long as you can. Grabbing the tube, I stepped in front of the full-length mirror hanging on the back of the bathroom door. Seeing myself completely put together I had mixed thoughts. On one hand, I thought I did look pretty amazing. In fact, I wasn't sure if my breasts had ever looked better. On the other hand, I worried I looked too sexy. Maybe I was sending William the wrong message. Hell, I wasn't even sure at this point what message I wanted to be sending.

I knew I missed being touched. I looked at other couples, the way they touched, and kissed—the most basic level of interaction—and I missed it. No matter how hard I tried to tell myself not to miss it, I did. I wanted it again, and I also wished I didn't want it. It was too hard, too complicated, too messy. In that moment I wished I were *that* type of girl. A girl who could seek out pleasure from a man and it not mean love. I wanted to be a girl who could have a one night stand, quench that fire and move on with my life with no complications.

Twisting up the tube I watched as the blush-colored lipstick rose from its hiding place. Applying the color to my top lip, I was suddenly interrupted by a knock at the door. I finished, pressing my lips together firmly, flattened out the dress over my abdominal area, and with a deep huff I turned to welcome my date. *God, what the hell are you doing, girl?*

Initially I struggled to walk in the heels, but after a few steps my legs remembered how to accommodate the shoes. Walking through the kitchen, I turned the doorknob slowly, my heart beginning to race. Pulling it open, my heart fluttered as I saw Colin Bennett standing there. His arm was perched above him on the doorframe, his head hanging down. He raised an eyebrow as he drank me in, one side of his mouth lifted into a sinister smile.

Damn it! Why did he have to look so damn sexy when he was being so dirty? I knew exactly what he was thinking as he was looking at me. He must have had plans; well, he was wearing a black button up shirt, only the top button undone, a lean cut charcoal gray blazer over it, hugging close to his body. My eyes moved down to his black slacks and vintage suede leather shoes. His hair was pushed back, a few wild strands hanging in his eyes. I felt an ache deep within me, which only made me want to slap him, even though I knew it wasn't his fault I was starting to lose control of my body.

"What do you want?" I asked, turning and walking away, leaving the door hanging open. I knew if I looked at him standing there any longer I might lose it. Why did he have to look so good? I suppose the jerks always did.

"Damn," he whispered softly, not moving from his perch. I couldn't help but smile as I continued moving away from him. I was glad I had garnered that sort of reaction; at least the dress was doing its job. I just hoped it would do the same for William.

"Do you need something?" I asked looking over my shoulder, making sure he didn't see his response pleased me.

Colin pulled his arm down, and following me into the apartment, he closed the door behind him. I grabbed my clutch from the couch and dropped the tube of lipstick in, turning and looking back at him for some sort of answer to my question. He was still staring at me intensely, like an animal that wanted to devour its prey.

"Christian told me to meet him here," Colin explained at last.

"What? No, that can't be right. Paige already left to meet up with him. They were going to some party, I think," I enlightened him.

"I know, apparently it was lame. He called and told me to meet him here. We're going to The Half King instead. I'd invite you, but it appears you already have a wild night planned for yourself." He smiled mischievously, and I could tell exactly what he was insinuating.

"Well, they're not here," I replied, refusing to give his last comment any sort of acknowledgment. Time was ticking by quickly, and I wanted to get Colin out of the apartment before William showed up. The last thing I needed to explain was why he was at my place.

"So, 'not-interested-in-dating-right-now,' where are you going dressed up like that?" he inquired, making himself comfortable in the oversized chair near the window. I couldn't believe he actually had the nerve to ask me that, and even worse, to throw my own words back up in my face. A week ago I had no intention of dating anyone. Hell, right now I had no intention of dating anyone. I wasn't about to tell him I was horny and a hot guy asked me out so I caved. I thought I sounded like a slut for just thinking it.

"I don't really think it's any of your business where I'm going." I nervously looked back at the door; I needed to figure out how to get him out.

"I suppose not, but I think it's obvious by the way you look you're going on a date. The question is, why lie to me about not wanting to date right now?" Colin pushed; the line of questioning was clearly a thrill for him.

"It's dinner, not that big a deal." I dismissed his statement, not allowing him to see how much he was getting under my skin.

"Well, you look amazing, Em," Colin complimented in a deep and irresistible voice. I couldn't stop staring at his beard—it always seemed to be kept at the perfect length of slight stubble. I was certain it was smooth enough to not irritate you when you kissed, but long enough to accentuate his strong jawline. *Damn it Clementine! Quit thinking like that!*

"Thanks. But like I said, they're not here, so I guess you should head home and try calling him perhaps," I urged, desperate for him to leave.

"I'm fine. I'll just wait here for them... if you don't mind. You can keep me company," Colin replied, looking me up and down again.

"Actually—" I began, but then was interrupted.

"Oh, wait, I get it. You don't want me here when your date gets here," Colin said, clasping his fingers together, watching me intensely from the chair. "What is it? Is he ugly? No wait, he's old... like really old, right?"

"Excuse me?" I growled as he laughed, trying not to laugh myself.

"That's it, isn't it?" Colin leaned forward, still laughing. "You're into the geriatric dudes aren't you?"

"No!" I exclaimed, chuckling slightly. "He's actually very hot."

Why are you talking to him? I asked myself. He's just playing you. It's what he does. Closing my eyes for a moment I took a deep breath, focusing on the task before me: getting Colin the hell out of my place before William showed up.

"Sweetheart, I was just playing around. I'm sure he's a great guy." Colin smiled as he attempted to soften the blow of his earlier teasing. I didn't have time to respond, because in the next moment there was a knock at the door.

It was too late. I had run out of time. I turned away from Colin to answer it. I needed to think quickly. I would open the door and slip out so there would be no time for William and Colin to meet. Pulling back my shoulders, I pushed the air from my lungs, opening the door. As I did, I heard Colin's voice... directly behind me.

"Don't worry, he'll think you look as hot as I do." He was standing so close I could feel his breath on my neck. What the hell? Was he some sort of stealthy vampire? How in the heck did he sneak up on me so quickly? It was too late now; the door was already open. My jaw had dropped, my mouth hanging open from Colin's comment.

William stood there looking at me with flowers in his hand. They were a beautiful array of wild flowers, but I could say nothing, only look back at him, expressionless. Colin was directly behind me—his breath still finding its way to my bare back.

"Hi," Colin greeted him, reaching past me and extending a hand to my date. "I'm Colin Bennett. You must be the date."

I couldn't believe my ears. He was really doing this, and I was just standing there like an idiot, letting him.

William hesitated for a moment, obviously puzzled, a

nervous half smile emerging. At last he freed a hand, and the two locked in a shake. "Yes, I suppose I am the date. Name is Stryker, William Stryker."

As he pulled his hand back, Colin burst out into a robust laughter before asking, "Like Bond? James Bond? Sorry, friend, I don't mean anything, that's just, well— that's quite a name."

William looked annoyed. I remembered when we were at the park, and how he mentioned he had been made fun of for his name while growing up. Leave it to Colin to alienate a guy in the first thirty seconds of meeting him. "I'm sorry, who are you?"

With an elbow to Colin's ribs, I managed to block any answer from him as he gasped in response. Any reply he had would probably be dripping with sarcasm and only create an uncomfortable evening for William and I. "Nobody important. Tell Paige I'll be back late."

I grabbed the flowers with a smile, remarking how beautiful they were and what a thoughtful gesture it was. Shoving them into Colin's hands, I slipped through the door and pulled it closed behind me.

As we walked down the stairs, I knew what was coming. There was no way any guy would let slide what just happened. There would be questions.

"Who was that?" he asked. And there it was. I had expected to make it out onto the sidewalk before the questions began, however, William clearly was one not to beat around the bush.

"My landlord," I answered plainly, as if it were quite inconsequential to me. Yes, he was a super hot landlord, and he also made me want to strangle him sometimes, but William didn't ask me those questions.

William shook his head as he followed me out into the night. "Wait, what? Does he live with you?"

I knew I would not be able to avoid the questions with a dismissive attitude and decided if I wanted any chance at a fun evening I would need to clear the air quickly. I stopped and turned to look at him.

"God, no! My roommate Paige is dating Colin's brother. He was there waiting for them. I don't know, I think they're all going out or something." There, I had explained, it and it didn't sound as insane as I thought it would. "So, where to?"

"Is he an ex or something?" William continued to push for answers.

"What? No way! Gross! Colin is not the type of guy I would ever date," I informed him, clueless as to what would ever give him the idea there had been something between us at one time.

"Really? He seems nice enough, and I suppose good looking, if you like that drop dead gorgeous type thing." I needed this conversation about Colin to end... and quickly. He was the last person I wanted to be thinking about.

"I guess... I never really noticed..." I lied. I wasn't interested in dating Colin, but anyone with a set of eyeballs could see he was gorgeous.

"Are you hungry?" William asked, my answer seeming to satisfy his curiosity.

"Famished," I replied with a smile, linking my arm into his.

"You look beautiful, by the way." I was pleased to have him confirm Colin's sentiments. Here I was, on my first date since—well, that's not important. I was ready for a fresh start.

CHAPTER 8

*T*he light peeked through the slatted wood blinds in my bedroom. Morning apparently did not care that I had stayed out late—it was determined to come upon me, no matter what. I begrudgingly drug myself to the bathroom sink, the picture of the girl in the mirror shocking me. In my late night semi drunken stupor, I had made my way to my bedroom, slipping out of the borrowed dress and climbed into bed.

My morning breath was offensive, mascara was caked on under my eyes, and if the raccoon look wasn't bad enough, my hair was a veritable rat's nest. Staring at the sexy black underwear, I couldn't imagine what I must have been thinking when I put them on.

Splashing my face with some warm water, I lathered up and rinsed away a few of the traces of the previous night, using my wet fingers to comb through my hair. Pulling the tangles up, I placed the matted hair into a loose and feeble attempt at a ponytail. A toothbrush hanging from my mouth, I walked out and searched my drawers for sweat pants and one of Ashton's oversized t-shirts. This had become my uniform for bumming it since as long as I could remember.

Walking back into the bathroom, spitting and rinsing, I flicked off the light, shaking my head in disappointment at myself. A cup of coffee and bowl of cereal would make everything better, I decided. Attempting to be as quiet as possible, I cracked my door open. I held my breath, but it did not seem to lessen the creaking under my feet. The last thing I needed this morning was the third degree from Paige about how the date had gone.

"About time!" I heard Paige call out from a reclined position on the couch. "I didn't think you'd ever get up."

I smiled. I should have known she would be waiting for me. "Good morning."

"Morning? I don't know what clock you've looked at lately, but it's past noon, slut," Paige snarled, clearly pleased with her comments.

"Oh God, are you serious?" I asked in disbelief, still walking gently as I made my way to our small kitchen and began preparing my breakfast. As soon as I turned the corner I saw them—the flowers William, or should I say Stryker, brought me the night before. "Thanks for putting my flowers in water."

"I didn't do that," Paige replied, not the least bit curious about who did. I, on the other hand, immediately thought about it. It must have been Colin. I had been such a bitch to him last night; I couldn't believe he would take care of a gift a date brought me. Perhaps it was an unconscious gesture.

"I can't believe it's so late. I never sleep in like that," I noted, carrying my breakfast, or lunch rather, into the living room, taking a seat in the chair Colin had been perched in the night before. A thought flashed through my mind of how great he looked, but then I remembered all of his annoying little comments, and eagerly pushed any notion of him from my aching head.

"It's because you got home after me. Nobody ever gets in after me. So does that mean there was a walk of shame this morning?" Paige asked, sitting up and rubbing her hands together like she was waiting for something juicy and delicious.

"No," I mumbled with a full mouth, lowering my eyebrows in disgust.

"Oh, come on, roommate code, you have to give me all the dirty details, same as I have to give you all of mine," Paige informed me.

I swallowed and then smiled before explaining, "I don't want to know all your dirty details. Besides, I doubt I could handle them anyway, knowing you."

"Hey!" she started. "No, you're probably right. Christian and I can get very naughty."

"Agh! Gross. Stop! Please no more," I begged, lifting my shoulders up to block my ears from the offensive information.

"Fine, but I still want my half of roommate gossip. Was he fantastic in bed? A long schlong?" Paige's lips twisted into an evil curl at the ends, her eyes never leaving me.

I reached down with a free hand, grabbed a throw pillow from the floor, and launched it at her head. She caught it in the air, hugging it close to her body as she began laughing wildly. "You're terrible," I informed her.

"So it was tiny?" she continued.

"Oh my God, no, nothing happened," I insisted, continuing to eat my cereal.

"No, I don't accept that. There is no way you were out *that* late in *that* dress and nothing happened," Paige argued. "Spill it."

Oddly enough, there was something comforting in the idea of discussing it—something even more comforting in the idea of having a girlfriend. I hadn't had a real girlfriend since Laney. When I started seeing Ashton I inherited all of his friends, but they were always clearly loyal to him.

"Honestly? It started off pretty good. He took me to this great restaurant in Midtown," I began to retell the evening's events.

"Ooh! Where did you go?" Paige asked, absolutely panting with anticipation, savoring every detail.

"Some place called Gilt," I replied, remembering how impressed I was with the location and decor.

"Are you serious?"

"Umm—yeah, I mean, I think that's what it was called," I said, doubting my memory.

"That place is so expensive and posh! This guy must be loaded." Paige looked like she might leap from her seat with each piece of information I gave her.

"I don't know—maybe—he's some sort of investigator," I added.

"Well then he must have some dirt on some pretty powerful people," she suggested, giggling.

I smiled, "I doubt it's anything like that."

"If a guy took me to a place like that I would totally jump his bones," Paige informed me.

I gave her a disapproving look before reminding her of the boyfriend who she could barely detach her lips from. "I bet Christian would love to hear you say that."

"Maybe he should take me to some nicer places."

"Let's just say the restaurant was great, but the company, not so much," I offered, wanting to make sure she understood the evening was not as dreamy as she seemed to be imagining.

"What happened?"

"When we got there he had already ordered for us ahead of time. He told me he had asked the chef to prepare something special. At the time I was kind of amazed, but now, looking back on it, it was really annoying. The food was great, but it would have been nice if he had let me pick for myself," I explained.

"That doesn't sound like too terrible of an offense," Paige argued.

"Oh, just wait. So by like the millionth course he had had enough to drink to put down a buffalo, and he started talking about himself in the third person."

"No! He didn't!" she exclaimed.

"Yup! And it gets worse; he calls himself by his last name, which is Stryker. He proceeds to tell me about how 'Stryker has trouble with ladies getting too attached,' and 'Stryker always gets his man.'"

"Oh my God! I think I just vomited a little in my mouth."

"I know, right?" I squealed. "I ended up getting drunk just to be able to put up with him."

"So, why were you out so late? Where did you go?" Paige was clearly puzzled.

"Oh, this guy was a piece of work. He wouldn't let me leave. I told him I had to get up early, I had a headache, and at one point I even told him I had to wash my hair."

"Ouch."

Taking another bite I chewed, swallowed, and started laughing. Looking back on the night it was funny now.

"He didn't seem to take a hint," I added.

"Why didn't you just get up and leave?"

"I didn't want to be rude. I knew the place was expensive, and I had agreed to go on a date with him," I said, defending my actions.

"Oh, honey, you're a New Yorker now, you better learn to get rude."

I couldn't believe in only a week's time I had come to absolutely adore Paige. I was certain I couldn't have picked a better girl as my roommate. She always made me laugh, and I admired the way she lived her life exactly the way she wanted.

"I guess I do need to figure that out. Ugh, he seemed like such a nice guy when we were at the park. And he was hot, so damn hot!" The story felt even more ridiculous as I retold it. Paige was right; I could have saved the entire night by just getting up and walking out.

"The douchebags always are."

"He ended up dragging me all over the city, one club to the next, most of the night was a blur. He even flirted with other girls right in front of me, but I really didn't care by that point. I just wanted it to be over."

"At least you got a free dinner out of it," Paige said, attempting to point out the brighter side of the evening.

"Yeah, apparently if you pay a lot for dinner that must mean you will get laid. When he dropped me off he started groping me and trying to stick his disgusting tongue down my throat."

"Gross!"

"I know! I barely got out of his clutches; thank God we have a security door. I think he would have followed me all the way into the apartment had it not been there."

"No worries, I would have kicked his ass," Paige reassured, sticking up two fists and give me her best vicious facial expression. A deep belly laugh erupted from me at the image of her petite frame in the stance.

"I bet."

"I'm serious!" she defended her capabilities. "Okay, maybe I would have called Christian and Colin, and they would have come down here to kick his ass."

"Please, no. The last thing that night needed was for Colin to show up. He's such a pig." I rolled my eyes, leaning forward and placing the half empty bowl on the coffee table.

Paige looked at me, clearly perplexed by something I had said. "Why would you call him a pig?"

"You can't seriously be asking me that. You do remember I met Bailey, don't you?" I asked, eyebrows raised.

"That psychotic bitch? That's how you're making your judgment? She chased after Colin the entire time she lived here. He was never interested. She waited until he was totally wasted and then was all over him. He told her the next morning it was a mistake and even apologized to her —more than I think the whore deserved," Paige snarled.

"That's a little harsh, don't you think? I was drunk last night and managed not to sleep with my date. Seems like a lame excuse," I argued.

"Whatever. Colin and I argue sometimes, but that girl did everything she could to get her claws into him. I warned her to leave him alone, but she just wouldn't listen."

"He's so cocky, and I just think he's kind of a tool," I defended my position, avoiding her intense glare.

"Colin!" she exclaimed. "I don't think I have ever heard anyone describe Colin that way."

"Well, how would you describe him?" I asked, wanting to turn the heat away from myself.

"He's probably one of the most generous guys I have ever met. Take this apartment, for example: he charges me what it costs to break even on the loan," Paige explained.

"Whatever. He just does that because you're sleeping with his brother. If you two broke up, I bet he wouldn't be so generous," I insisted.

Immediately, I could tell I had gone too far. "You know, Emmie, you really shouldn't talk about things you know nothing about."

I should have shut up right there, but instead I went on the defensive. "Fine, enlighten me."

"There's a reason Colin doesn't have a girlfriend. He doesn't have time for one. His real estate business keeps him so busy that he can only make time for casual things, which he is always up front about with girls. I know a lot of guys who are not so honorable about the way they handle the same situations."

"Really, your defense of him being a player is because he is too busy making a lot of money? So, now he's shallow, too?" I argued, even more confident in my original stance.

"Do you know why Colin is driven to earn so much money?" I shook my head in response to her question. "When Colin was seventeen his parents were in a car crash, neither survived."

"Oh my God, that's terrible," I gasped. Looking at him you would have never known he had been through something so traumatic. Of course, I doubt many would guess my husband had killed himself.

"He and Christian moved in with their uncle, but that guy was completely useless. He was a videographer for some news station. He was never home. He never thought about who would get Christian off to school, or keep him out of trouble, or hell, even feed the poor kid. Do you think he made it to a single one of Christian's football games growing up? No. But Colin did. All Colin thought about was his brother. Christian was only ten when it happened, and as soon as Colin turned eighteen he filed for legal custody of him." I could see the respect now that Paige had for Colin. She admired him.

"That must have been hard on him," I agreed at last.

"It never ended for Colin. He could see their inheritance from the life insurance policies, which wasn't much, was dwindling fast, so when he was twenty, he took the last of it and bought his first investment property. I started dating Christian when he was sixteen, and the only thing I remember about those days is Colin either working or being with his brother. It's never changed much either."

"Are you serious? You've been with Christian that long?" I asked, a little shocked. I was certain by their behavior they were a new love.

"Yup, Christian tells me his whole life changed when he met me. It's hard to believe we've been together five and half years. God love him, he is hot as hell, but there is no way he would ever be able to hold down a real job. He was pretty messed up by his parents' death. Colin did the best he could with him, but he was just a kid, too."

"Well, you can't tell by looking at him. Christian seems to have it together."

"Oh my God, no," Paige said, flashing me a horrified look. "He's a hot mess. I have to take him to AA three times a week."

"Shut up!" I gasped in disbelief.

"I can party with the best of them, but Christian, he loses control. He doesn't know when to stop."

"I would have never guessed he had a problem like that."

Paige pushed her lips together into a thankful smile. "That's because of Colin. He gives up his own happiness to make sure his brother never has to worry about anything: money, a place to live, whatever it is, he tries to make sure he's taken care of. Don't get me wrong, Christian isn't lazy, he helps Colin with the work on the places. It's really sweet how much he looks up to his big brother. Sometimes, I don't know, though, it's like he checks out."

"I had no idea," I muttered, a wave of guilt washing

over me about the way I had judged Colin without actually getting to know him. It didn't change the fact that I thought his relationships with women were absolutely disgusting. But maybe I had been too hard on him.

"Yeah, I hope he hasn't bitten off more than he can chew," Paige added.

"What do you mean?"

"This warehouse conversion he's got himself tied up in. He had to pull money out of all of his other locations in order to secure the funds to buy the place. If he can't get an investor after the first unit is done, I'm not sure what they're going to do. He thinks Christian doesn't know, but he's not an idiot; he can see how worried Colin is."

It was becoming even clearer to me why Colin was so sensitive about the warehouse conversion. The future of both him and his brother were riding on it. I wished I hadn't said the things I did about it, but I had, and God, he must hate me.

"Enough of this depressing stuff," Paige said at last. "I just wanted you to know you should give Colin a chance. He's a really nice guy, and he thinks you're smoking hot, so there's that."

"What?" The word slipped from my lips in disbelief.

"He told me last night," Paige grinned.

"Oh." It was the only word I could manage to speak. I wasn't sure how I felt about this new piece of information. He never committed to women, which meant he was in fact a player, even if his motives were honorable. At the same time, he had been through so much heartbreak in his life, I could relate to that. Not that he would ever know my story.

"I almost forgot, Colin wanted to make sure I invited you to Half Kings next Saturday."

"What's Half Kings?" I inquired, remembering Colin mentioning it the night before, and trying to not think about the fact that Colin was asking about me.

"Some little hole in the wall a few blocks away. Colin leases them their space so he likes to hang out there."

"I don't get it, why would he want you to invite me?" My curiosity was too peaked not to ask.

"I think some band is playing or something. He thought you might enjoy it, I guess."

"We'll see." I pushed my tired body out of the chair, carrying my bowl to the sink to wash. "It's getting late, I need to get some work done for school."

I took refuge in my room with my art supplies. After a terrible date the night before, the last thing I wanted to think about was Colin... or any man for that matter. Escaping into a world with just my pencils and paper was exactly what the doctor ordered.

CHAPTER 9

I watched the boy as he visually sized up the oversized canvas. He looked at me, the canvas, then the small doorway, then back to me. "It's not going to fit lady."

"It will fit, let's try again," I insisted.

"It's eight and a half feet tall, so even if we got it through the doorway, it is not going up those stairs," he argued. I had never felt such contempt for a delivery boy, but this kid was really starting to get on my nerves.

"If you get it in there I'll give you an extra ten bucks." I said, attempting to bribe him.

"First off, it wouldn't matter if you gave me a thousand, it won't fit. Second, ten bucks, you can't be serious." The disapproving glare he gave me made me realize just how embarrassingly low my offer was. Yet another reason this kid was asking for a kick in the nuts.

"What seems to be the problem here?" Damn it! Colin.

"Nothing, we're fine," I said dismissively waving a

hand. It was too late; he had already spotted us and was only a few feet away now.

"She's insisting this will fit, and it won't. Look, I need to get back to the store. Do you need to return it, or do you have somewhere else you'd like me to take it?" the boy pushed, clearly as irritated as I was.

"No!" I exclaimed. "I need it, and if you would just try a little harder, I'm sure it would fit."

"Em, if he gets it through that door there is no way it will make it up the hall and into your apartment," Colin added.

"That's exactly what I told her, man, but she won't listen."

"Fine, we'll take it off the frame," I snapped, annoyed they were joining forces against me.

"Wait, why would you do that? You can keep it at the warehouse, where you're welcome to work on it whenever you need," Colin quickly offered with his ruggedly handsome half smile. Damn that smile.

"No," I answered. But nobody seemed to care what I said; the boy had already started to follow Colin with the canvas leaning against his body. I ran to catch up, pleading for them to stop. "No, really, that just won't be convenient. I need to be able to get in and work on it at all hours; it would just be too hard. That's why I didn't have them deliver it to the school."

"Nonsense, I'll give you a key," Colin said, holding the oversized door open for the kid.

I stopped for a moment, cocking my head, staring at Colin through squinted eyes. I couldn't figure out his end game. He had been so rude to me that first time we met, and every time since he seemed to delight in frustrating me. Why be so kind to me now?

Following the canvas through the door, I continued to try and plead my case, but Colin wouldn't hear it. I rode up in silence, attempting to think of other reasons this was not a good idea. The elevator came to a stop on the floor just above where I knew Colin's loft was. When the gates opened it set off a reaction, triggering the overhead lights automatically. Sprawling out before me was a vast and open warehouse space, random boxes and construction supplies strewn throughout.

"This floor has power so it should work for you," Colin explained, slipping some money into the delivery boy's hand.

"No, let me get that," I insisted, digging into my oversized pockets, but before I could turn around, the kid had closed the gate the car already lowering him out of site. "I wish you wouldn't have done that."

"Nonsense," Colin said, leaning the canvas against a nearby column. "It's business."

"Pardon me?" I asked, confused by his statement.

"After we talked the other day and you mentioned you sell your artwork I started doing some digging. I looked up your website, and I must say, your work is quite impressive," Colin praised.

"You what?" I asked, trying not to reveal how flattered and mortified I was. Apparently you can be both at the same time.

"I have a proposition for you." All right, I'll admit it. I'm not proud of the first thing that popped into my mind after he said that.

"Oh?"

"Yes, I would like to commission you to do some work for the space downstairs. I think it would be great to have some large pieces to hang in order to show off the high ceilings to the investors." When Colin proposed this, I felt a little embarrassed, and made a mental note to shame myself later. That was why he was suddenly being so nice to me. That was probably why he wanted me to go to the bar with them that weekend; he must have planned to ask me about this then.

"I don't know…" I hesitated. "I'm super busy with my assignments for school."

"Oh, please, I think they would be perfect. I can show you the colors of the room, and the rest is up to you. Complete artistic freedom, I promise." I hated to admit it, but the idea of being commissioned to do such large pieces was rather exciting for me. "You would also have a couple months to complete them… maybe longer. Depends on how the construction timeline goes. What about fifteen hundred a piece?"

My heart skipped a beat. That was an entire month's rent for each painting. While the size of the painting would justify the price, I had never made so much off a single one. *Don't let him see how giddy you are over the price, stupid*, I silently scolded myself.

"All right, but you have to buy my supplies," I agreed at last.

"Deal!" Colin exclaimed, clearly as excited as I was, not that he could tell from my reaction. I flashed a half smile, then thanked him for the use of the space. I could not have imagined a better studio space. On the far side of the room I had already spotted light coming in from a couple of street-facing windows. I could imagine where I would set up my table and perhaps a small area to sit.

"I'll leave you to it then. I'll have the supplies delivered to your workspace, and just let me know what you need when you get a chance." Colin pulled the lever, triggering the return of the lift. "Oh, and I'll have Christian drop a key off to you later. Let either of us know if you need anything else."

"I will, thank you," I said nodding my head.

I smiled as I watched him lower down into the darkness, waiting until he was completely out of sight before breaking out into a wild and gleeful dance. Twirling across the space, it felt like my heart might burst. I was in New York, living in an apartment, with an art studio, and now I had been commissioned to create paintings. Even if it was temporary, it was still one of the most amazing experiences I had ever had.

* * *

CHAPTER 10

*I*t was hard to believe that I'd only been living with Paige for a couple of weeks. My life had changed so much in such a short period of time; it often felt like I was living out someone else's reality. I was used to an existence where most of my thoughts were somehow consumed with guilt. The pain came every morning when I woke up. I wanted this new world to be real more than anything, to know the things I touched were actually part of my life.

Besides the occasional annoying call from Stryker, which I would never pick up, my days were full of excitement. I found out that each student in my studio painting class was expected to prepare a show over the semester. After we submitted our portfolios the professor will choose a few students to show at a gallery in town. While many spots were to show your work on campus there were a few bigger gallery spots being reserved for an elite selection of students. I was determined to be one of those chosen for this privilege.

I spent that first night in the studio space painting, losing all track of time. I only managed to eke out a few hours of sleep. Tuesday went much like Monday, and I was starting to wonder if I would be able to find any time for sleeping, but apparently my body decided three days was my limit of sleepless abuse. I had crawled into bed Wednesday night—well, I suppose it was Thursday morning actually—for my small amount of sleep, and before I knew it, I woke up… just before noon. I panicked, realizing I had missed most of my classes for the day.

Once I had a little coffee and food I was much calmer about the situation. I probably shouldn't have felt that way, but I was rather excited I got the entire day to paint in my amazing studio. In no way would I ever admit this to Colin because I could just imagine his smug expression of satisfaction. I had half expected him to show up every day, checking up on me. Much to my surprise, I hadn't seen him since the night he made me the job offer. When I arrived Tuesday, the canvas I needed for his pieces was waiting for me. No note—they were simply leaning up against the wall in the area I had been working.

Bounding down the stairs, even I had to admit I noticed there was an extra skip in my step. When I was younger it was like I had a soundtrack to my life, playing in my head, but I had lost that rhythm so long ago, it was hard to remember it. It was coming back to me, and I often found myself smiling while I walked, humming a tune only I could hear.

Pulling the lift gate closed behind me I made my way over to my work area. The flowers I had placed in a mason jar by the window on Monday were already starting to droop. Plucking one of the few unwilted daisies from the collection I secured it behind my ear. Shoving my iPhone onto the docking station I gleefully pressed play on my favorite Pandora station I had lovingly entitled "*folksy*." Of Monsters and Men began echoing throughout the vast space.

Picking up my brush, I proceeded to turn the music up as high as it would go. With one sweep of the brush, and then another, I was there, in the moment, blissfully happy with what I was doing. A joy, so intense it made my heart ache as it filled me up.

My body gave way to the feelings, my full hips swaying from side to side. I raised my arms above my head and began to sing as if I were alone in the shower. Bringing one arm down with a tremendous swipe at the canvas, then another, a fluid dance enveloped me.

I didn't notice the world around me; it was simply the art, the music, and me. At least until the song ended. Much to my surprise the momentary silence between songs gave way to the loud applause of an onlooker. I spun around, clutching my paint covered brush to my chest. Colin stood, leaning against a concrete column, and from the smirk he was perfectly wearing, I was certain he had seen the entire display. Though I was mortified, he was clearly quite satisfied with what he had witnessed.

Even though I wanted to march over and punch him in the chest, wiping that smug grin off his face, I refused to give him the satisfaction. Instead, I somehow managed to muster up a laugh... better to join him, I suppose. I rushed over, pausing my playlist.

"Nice moves," he said, standing upright.

"Why thank you," I replied, avoiding direct eye contact.

"No, really I mean it. I particularly enjoyed the rotating hip action you had going there. Very spicy."

"Is there something you needed?" I questioned, eager to stop his taunting as well as to return to my painting. Damn, I did it. I made eye contact. The steely gray of them always managed to lock me in.

"Oh yeah, sorry. I guess you had me all hot and bothered by your dance moves. The reason for my visit nearly slipped my mind." Colin's suggestive tone sent a chill down my spine. Turning around and taking a few steps toward the lift he yelled, "Bring it in, boys."

With that, the entire floor became a bustling hive. Half a dozen men were scurrying about as I stood there speechless, watching the scene unfold before me, helpless.

"Over by that window—that's where she likes to work," Colin bellowed.

"What is going on?" I finally managed to ask, staring at him, my jaw still agape.

Two burly men made their way past me muttering a pardon and excuse me. They carried a deep red velvet couch with ornate dark colored wood to the area where two other men had just unrolled an oversized black carpet. The remaining workers brought in what appeared to be floodlights, making quick work of running the power cords.

"I know you've been working really hard and had some late nights, so I thought I would make the place a little more comfortable for you. It seemed like the least I could do," Colin explained.

"And somehow you thought I would be comfortable in a place decorated like the littlest whore house in Texas?" I asked, staring at the set up in disbelief. The entire incident was absurd; this couldn't be happening.

Looking back at Colin, he seemed to be ignoring my comments as he slipped some cash into one of the men's oversized hands.

"Did you hear me? They need to take it all back," I commanded.

But no one was listening, and the men were loaded into the lift before the words made their way completely out of my mouth, leaving just Colin and me standing there, surrounded by some of the tackiest furniture I might have ever seen.

"I don't think it's that bad, just give it a try. I thought it was actually quite comfortable," Colin pleaded, walking over to the sofa.

"Do you understand what I do here? First of all, this stuff will just end up with paint all over it. It makes no sense. You make no sense. I mean seriously, what were you thinking?" I scolded. I was there, using that space because I wanted to paint, not entertain guests.

"Hear me out," Colin began, lowering his head as if he were trying to avoid direct eye contact with a wild animal. "I know you've been here late the last few nights—"

"And how do you know that? Are you spying on me? Because if you are I don't think this is going to work. I mean it, I won't put up with your crap," I snapped, surprising even myself with my reaction.

"Dear God, woman! Calm the hell down." Colin no

longer bowed his head; instead, he had taken a couple steps toward me, his face only inches from mine. "Will you listen for a minute? I'm usually up late working downstairs. I can hear the lift when you leave, so sorry to burst your bubble, but no, I'm not stalking you. I have better things to do with my time. As for the furniture, yes I know what you do here, but this stuff is from a salvage job my crew did on a building I bought. It may not be fashionable, but it was clean, looked comfortable, and I didn't care if you covered it in paint since I can't really use it for staging. Sorry if the style isn't to your liking, but I was just trying to do something nice."

I wondered if I would ever be able to unhinge my jaw far enough to pull my foot out. What was I thinking? Perhaps that he was bringing a couch in so that he could ravage me. He had no such intentions; he was simply being a nice guy, and I tore into him like some mad woman. Looking over my shoulder I considered making a run for the exit, but then decided it would be pointless.

"Colin, I'm so sorry."

"Look, I can keep my distance if that's what you want," Colin offered, taking a few steps toward the lift.

"No, wait, please!" I exclaimed. What was I doing? He thought I was a crazy bitch; this was the perfect way to eliminate a possible distraction from my life... if I could just keep my mouth shut.

Colin turned and looked at me, raising an eyebrow, waiting for me to say something that would change his mind.

"Don't go. I completely overreacted. Can we start over?" And there it was—I took my chance of getting rid of this gorgeous guy and completely threw it out the window.

He glared at me, as if he were trying to figure me out. I could have told him that was useless, because hell, I didn't even know what I was doing half the time. "Only if you try the couch out?"

I watched as Colin ran to where the parlor style sofa sat. He leaped over the back with both legs and landed at one end with a bounce. I couldn't help but laugh. Sometimes he seemed so full of life, I envied him. "You're crazy!"

Patting the area next to him, he beckoned me over, "Come on, if you want to make nice, you have to try it out."

With a deep breath I walked over to the sofa, making my way around the opposite end, slowly taking a seat. He watched intensely, waiting for my response. I looked at him seriously, determined not to give him any indication of my opinion.

"Well?" he begged.

I collapsed backward, throwing my arms out to my side. "All right, fine! I'll admit it, the whore house couch is the most damn comfortable piece of furniture I have ever sat on."

"I told you!" he exclaimed, falling back, and we both laughed.

When a silence settled over us, I stretched out a bare toe and used it to restart the previously paused music, adjusting the volume with the same big toe.

"That might be a marketable skill," Colin noted, impressed.

"What?"

"The foot thing," he said.

"Oh," I laughed for a moment. "That's nothing, I can also pick things up with my feet."

"I knew something was different about you the moment I saw you… now I finally know what it was."

"You got me," I confessed. "I used to travel with a circus, but after things ended poorly with me and the bearded lady I was forced to find refuge elsewhere."

"Sometimes love can be tough," Colin offered with a slight grin. It was weird, even though I thought he was disgusting when it came to women, I was very comfortable with him.

"I don't blame her… it was tough after she caught me with the fat lady," I pushed, wondering how far I could take it before he ceased to see the humor.

"It's all right, we all need a little chunk now and then. You know what they say, more cushion for the pushin'." I wondered how he managed to say it with a completely serious look on his face. Leaning across the couch I shoved him in the chest, bursting out into a deep laughter.

"You're not right!" I exclaimed.

"Hey, you started it," he defended himself, waving his arms in front of him, attempting to call a truce on the physical assault.

"Seriously, though, this was really sweet of you. I'm sorry I wigged out. You didn't have to do this."

"I thought if I made this place comfortable enough, maybe you would stay here all night and actually paint some stuff for me." I appreciated the way he tried to lighten the awkwardness of the moment.

"Oh, is that right?"

"Yeah, so when are you going to work on my stuff?" Colin asked, his sarcasm evident in his tone.

"Maybe by Christmas." I grinned.

His face shifted momentarily, clearly surprised by my answer. "What?"

"I'm kidding. Now who needs to lighten up?"

He smiled. "All right, you got me."

"I have some ideas, so I should be able to show you some early stage pieces by next week. Will that work for you?"

"Yeah, that would be awesome."

We both sat quietly as a Bon Iver song began to play in the background. I stared at my class project, briefly looking over at Colin, who I noticed was also gazing at the work.

"You know, I don't normally let people see my work in progress. I might have to kill you now."

Colin didn't laugh at my snarky remark. Instead, he continued to look at the piece. He stood, examining the strokes more closely. I suddenly felt very self-conscious, as if I were naked on an exam table.

"Is there something wrong?" I searched, no longer able to stand the silence between us.

"Huh?" Colin huffed over his shoulder.

"Is there something wrong with the painting?" I asked again, standing and moving next to him.

"Oh, no, not at all. Sorry, I was just looking at it," Colin replied, not taking his eyes off the piece.

"You hate it, don't you?" I asked, already sure of what he was thinking.

"No, I just see something different in this one than in your other work I saw online," Colin explained.

"Like what?"

"Oh, nothing," he said, turning to walk away.

I grabbed his arm, spinning him back around. He was crazy if he thought I would let him leave after that kind of statement. "I don't think so, buddy. You can't say something like that and walk away. Spill it. I can take it."

I could see his hesitation, and it made me even more anxious. This was why I didn't want people to see my work before it was ready. "Your work, it's different."

"What do you mean? Different than what?" I pushed, even though I was unsure I wanted to hear the answer.

"When I saw your work online, I don't know, there was a sadness to it. This one is different, though. There's so much vibrancy and movement. It's—it's different."

"I can't tell if you think that's a good or bad thing," I said giving him a slight playful shove in the arm.

"No, don't get me wrong, I like it. It's beautiful, actually."

"Don't sound so surprised," I jested, my insides smiling secretly from his praises.

"All right, all right," he said laughing and stumbling closer to the lift. "Clearly you're determined to give me a hard time, so I'll let you get back to work."

"Yeah, you do that," I called out after him, not moving from the spot where I stood.

"Oh yeah, you're coming this weekend, right?" he asked as the gate hovered above his extended arm.

"This weekend?"

"Half Kings? Don't tell me Paige forgot to tell you."

I didn't know what to say. I simply assumed Paige had exaggerated when she said Colin wanted me to come. "No, she told me. I'm just really busy with school."

"Nonsense, I want you to be there, so you're coming." Before I could respond, the gate was closed, and the lift had begun to move. I wasn't sure why he wanted me to go so badly, but even more so I couldn't figure out why I wanted to go now.

CHAPTER 11

Paige ground the chips between her teeth so loudly I could hear it over the music. Looking over my shoulder I stared at her for a moment. I wasn't sure how this small, frail being could possibly consume as many calories as she did in any given day and yet remain so petite. It was starting to annoy me, because all I could think about was grabbing that bag of black pepper and sea salt kettle chips from her delicate little hands and stuffing my face with them. I knew for me, however, it would mean not being able to button my jeans for the next week if I even stared too long at the delicious treat.

"You know, you can wait for me at the apartment. I won't be that much longer," I offered, more for my own sanity than hers.

"Yeah right," she mumbled with bits of chip flying from her mouth, finding their way into the fibers of the black carpet. "You said that like an hour ago. If I leave you here, you will never go tonight."

"What does it matter if I go?" I asked, unsure of why my presence was so important.

"Colin asked me to bring you, and I promised him I would," Paige explained, shrugging her shoulders as if to say she were simply the innocent messenger.

"I don't get it. Why does Colin care so much if I go?" I investigated, not wanting to let on that I missed seeing him. It had been two days since he brought me the furniture. I had considered, on several occasions, making an excuse to stop in at his loft.

"I don't know—" Paige replied, her eyes suddenly widening.

"What is it?"

"Oh my God, you like him, don't you?" She gasped. How on earth could she sense such a thing from what I had said? Not that I did like him...

"What? Are you crazy?"

"No, you are. You've got it bad for him."

"I'm not doing this. You're certifiable," I replied, dropping my soiled brush into the nearby bucket. Wiping my hands on a rag, I retrieved my iPhone and slid it into my pocket.

"You do! That's why you're avoiding the question." Paige sat up quickly, watching me as I paced around the space like a caged animal.

"I don't know what you're talking about," I insisted.

Paige stood and started to walk away from me toward the lift. "Fine, if you say so. But I think he's got it just as bad for you."

"What?" I cried, freezing.

"If you don't like him, though, I guess that doesn't

matter." It was too late, Paige had me in her tight little grasp. I followed closely behind, trying to fish out any small detail of what she might be talking about.

"I don't care, but what would make you say something like that?" I asked, following her all the way out to the street and back to our apartment.

"Yeah, you don't care, whatever. He asks about you every time I see him," Paige explained.

I thought about the evidence for a moment, quickly deciding it was flimsy at best. "I'm your roommate, of course he is going to ask about me."

"Then why has he asked me like ten times if you're coming tonight? Please, you two are so obvious. Better hurry, we're leaving in thirty minutes." Paige laughed, walking into her bedroom and pushing the door closed in my face.

I rushed into my bathroom without another word. Paige's notions running through my head, I wasn't sure how I felt about this revelation. Perhaps outraged... I mean he could have been playing me all along. Maybe the sofa and his kind behavior recently was just a ploy to get me to let my guard down. I wondered what his lips felt like. Wait, this was not why I was here; look how things went with Stryker. He was a complete loon, and even worse, I couldn't get away from Colin—he was my land-lord and now an employer. This was very bad idea.

Stepping into the steam-filled shower, my body tingled, the hot water rushing over my nakedness. Before I even realized what was happening, an image of Colin popped into my head. I thought of the day we met and his shirtless body. As the steam danced around me, I remembered the feeling of his breath on my shoulder. *Damn it, Em!* I scolded myself. *Snap out of it!*

Stepping from the shower stall, I quickly dried off, then used the towel to wipe away the moisture on the bathroom mirror. I had huge dark circles under my eyes, and my hair had become a kinky, frizzy mess. I didn't have much of a choice based on how little time I had. I pulled my hair up into a high ponytail, allowing a few strategic strands to encircle my face. Once my makeup was applied I actually started to think I looked human again.

There was a knock at my bedroom door. "Five minutes, Emmie," Paige warned.

Without a word in response, I darted to my closet. There wasn't time to search through Paige's wardrobe for the one or two things that might fit me. I would somehow have to find something in my own closet that made me look good. My fingertips grazed over a red summer dress that was covered in a white paisley-like pattern. It would have to do. Slipping it on, I quickly realized the cleavage was a bit on the extreme side so I grabbed my cropped jean jacket and threw it on top.

Searching my closet further, I pulled out my favorite pair of brown cowboy boots, which had a lot of character from years of wear. I placed them on my feet and then stared in the mirror. I could only imagine the taunting that would ensue when Paige saw me, but it was what I had to work with. I turned and took a deep breath, opening the door and walking into the living room, closing my eyes, bracing myself for the snickering.

I waited, hearing nothing. I opened my eyes. Paige

stood in front of me, still looking me up and down—examining me. At last she simply noted, "Cute. Let's go."

Seriously? Paige always had something horrible to say about everything I wore. Did she actually just say I looked cute? I thought in that moment I might have a heart attack, but that thought quickly faded to relief for the hope that I actually did look cute... and I would look cute when Colin saw me. Not that it mattered.

* * *

When we arrived at the bar Paige explained we were only a "fashionably" thirty minutes late so it wouldn't be a big deal. Personally, I never understood the term. As far as I was concerned, late was late, and it meant you didn't respect my time. I kept quiet, however, assuming Paige must know of these matters in New York better than I.

I followed closely behind her; I could feel my heart starting to race. I had seen Colin dozens of times before this, and I couldn't figure out why all of the sudden the prospect of it made my head spin. It didn't help that Paige was filling it with all of these notions that Colin might actually be interested in me romantically.

"Em, you look great." I heard Colin's deep voice behind me. Quickly I spun around, where he was now only inches away from me. Paige wasted no time leaping into Christian's arm and beginning the make out session. I figured after being apart for hours, for Paige it felt like being deprived of oxygen. They were enough to make a girl want to vomit.

"Thanks," I replied with a sideways grin. "Jesus, you would think they'd not seen each other for a year," I commented, nodding toward the lovebirds.

Colin laughed, but didn't take his eye off me. "I'm really glad you came tonight. I think you'll really like this band."

"Oh yeah?" I asked, the hair on my arms standing up on end. *He's just some guy*, I told myself firmly and silently.

Giving Christian a slap to the back of the head, Colin managed to tear him away from Paige for a moment, allowing the four of us to make our way to a booth near the edge of the stage. We continued to talk to one another for a few moments about my painting, about his renovation work, and I found myself wishing there was no band. I loved music, and I had never wanted to talk to someone more than I wanted to listen to music, but amazingly enough, Colin managed to change that in me. He was genuinely interesting, though he could never know I thought so.

"Do you want a drink?" he asked, standing and looking down at me.

"Sure. Whatever is fine with me," I answered. Our gazes lingered for a moment, and I could feel an ache between my legs.

"Colin Bennett!" A high-pitched squeal came from across the bar. All of us turned in sync and looked to the source. Running toward our booth was a woman in a miniskirt and blouse tied up in a knot below her ample bosom. Her skin looked as though she might have fallen asleep in a tanning bed on more than one occasion, and her hair was so black it glistened even in the dim light of the bar.

Without hesitation the girl threw her arms around Colin and began passionately kissing him. Based on the amount of tongue she was delivering with the greeting they were no strangers. My stomach turned inside out, and I worried I might actually get sick.

I hopped to my feet and made my way around the outside of the booth. Colin broke away from the grasp of the girl and delivered a horrified stare in my direction. I looked down at Paige who looked equally horrified for me.

"Hey girl," my voice trembled as I spoke, "I have a lot to get done, so I really should get going."

I didn't wait for an answer, and I didn't turn around as I heard Colin calling out after me. In fact, I didn't stop until I was all the way back home, in my room, with the door locked behind me.

I don't know how I could have been so stupid. I knew who Colin was from the moment I met him, yet somehow I let myself be fooled. I didn't know how I would avoid him moving forward, but I did know I couldn't see him right now. I would deal with it when I had to, but for now I didn't want to think about anything that had to do with Colin Bennett.

Slipping my dress off and letting it fall to the floor I pulled on one of Ashton's oversized shirts. It was sad, but familiar, and I could handle familiar.

CHAPTER 12

* * *

"Seriously, Emmie, you're going to have to talk to him at some point," Paige argued, walking around the couch and handing me a cup of coffee.

"No, I don't. I see absolutely no point in talking to him," I replied firmly.

"I told you, he and Courtney are long over," Paige attempted to reassure me.

"It didn't look long over," I retorted. "And honestly, I'm not interested in Colin so it doesn't even matter."

"Yeah, you're not into Colin, whatever you say." Paige delivered a scowl before rolling her eyes. "Courtney used to be a waitress there, and they dated for a very short time. She's just one of those type of girls, ya know?"

"The fact that you just said she's one of those type of girls, and I assume you mean slutty, makes it all the more horrifying. There is no way I would ever be interested in a guy who would date a girl like that," I explained, holding my head high.

"Well then, you better settle on never finding love,

because all men are interested in that type of girl at one time or another in their lives."

"Fine, then I'll be alone. I don't really need a guy to be happy. Some girls are content to be alone," I insisted as my phone buzzed.

"Whatever you say. You just keep telling yourself that." She scoffed at my statement.

I groaned as I saw Stryker's number scrolling across my screen. This guy did not give up easily.

"Is it *him* again?" Paige asked, her face displaying a look of utter shock.

"Yes, he can't take a hint. I saw him at the school the other day and had to hide out in a classroom for nearly twenty minutes. I wish I had never agreed to go out with him. Dating and me simply do not mix."

"Oh my God, why don't you just tell him you're not interested and that he needs to go get a life?" she suggested. "Better yet, tell him you're screwing Colin."

"Okay, first of all, gross," I said, raising a finger and waving it around to prove my point. "I would never screw Colin. Second—"

We both paused, interrupted by a knock at the door. "Hey babe, let us in."

"Us?" I whispered, clearly agitated, rising up onto my knees, staring intensely at Paige.

"What? I invited them over for a movie night before I knew you were all hung up on Colin," she replied casually, walking over to the door.

"Don't you let him in here, Paige!" I whisper yelled, stressing my discomfort with the situation quite plainly.

"I'll make sure he leaves you alone, all right?" she said,

not waiting for my response. Quickly, I slouched down on the sofa, pulling the throw pillow up to my chest as if it were a shield.

"Hey boys," Paige said, cracking the door. "Whoa, not so quick. You guys can come in tonight, but we have a few ground rules."

"Ground rules?" Just the sound of Colin's voice made my stomach do flips. I kept seeing that Courtney girl sticking her tongue down his throat over and over.

"Yes, ground rules. You got a problem with that?" Paige sternly questioned, not budging.

"Was this Em's idea?" Colin asked.

"No!" I yelled from the couch. "My idea was to not let you in at all."

"Can't we at least talk about it?" Colin yelled from the doorway.

"Nothing to talk about!" I hollered back.

"Look boys, the rules are no talking about anything that happened last night, deal?" Paige offered, holding the door firmly.

"Whatever," Christian muttered, pushing his way in.

"You can't be serious," Colin moaned, clearly not in agreement with the rules.

"As a heart attack, my friend," Paige replied.

"Fine." I heard him sigh. A wave of relief washed over me, and I was suddenly very glad I had Paige looking out for me.

"Great, you boys make the popcorn," she commanded as the door closed. Rushing over, she took the spot next to me on the couch, grabbing my hand and squeezing it tightly. I knew for the first time in a very long time, I truly had a close friend—a friend I could trust.

A minute later my phone began to buzz again.

"Oh my God, you are kidding me, right? It's not him, is it?" Paige snarled with disgust.

Looking down at the phone, I saw it was, in fact, another attempt from William Stryker. Begrudgingly, I nodded. "At least this time he only sent a text."

"What did he say?" she asked, swiping at my phone.

"Nothing."

"Oh please, I know it's not nothing. Let me see!" she exclaimed.

I handed her the phone, making sure I didn't make eye contact with Colin during any part of the conversation. I could feel him hovering over our shoulders, spying on our conversation.

"Oh, no he didn't," she remarked before beginning to feverishly run her fingers over the screen of my phone, typing a message that I was sure wouldn't lead to anything good.

"What are you typing?" I asked, but she didn't answer, too intensely engaged in her message. "I'm serious, Paige, don't. Please don't."

"Too late," she replied, tossing me the phone, satisfaction across her face. "He won't be bothering you again."

"What did you do?" I asked, panic flooding through me.

"Only what needed to be done. That douchebag sounded like he was threatening you," Paige defended herself.

"Someone is threatening you?" Colin asked, pushing himself into the conversation.

"No, it's nothing I can't handle," I replied firmly.

"He said you better quit ignoring me... or else," Paige reported.

"What? Who is saying this stuff to you?" Colin was quickly becoming agitated.

"Nobody," I insisted, wishing the conversation would drop.

"I told him if he contacted you again, I'd cut his balls off and feed them to him," Paige proudly announced.

"That's my classy lady," Christian said, smiling as he handed Paige a beer, a ginger ale in his other hand for himself.

"Damn straight, and I would do it," she reaffirmed.

"Who is saying this stuff?" Colin said in a now very demanding tone. His intense stare was starting to make me extremely uncomfortable.

"That dick head she went on that date with," Paige so graciously enlightened the boys.

"Wait, that guy calling himself Stryker?" Colin attempted to clarify.

"Oh my God, Paige! Shut up! And yes, it's him, but I'm telling you all, I've got this. Just let me handle it. If I ignore him long enough, he'll go away," I maintained.

Colin made his way around the couch, kneeling uncomfortably close to me. In a low voice he said, "Em, I'm not kidding, if he bothers you anymore, will you promise to tell me, and I'll take care of it."

"Look, I said I'm fine." I adjusted awkwardly in my seat.

"Promise me!" Colin commanded, staring at me

intensely. "I don't trust that guy. Something didn't feel right. Will you please promise me?"

"All right, fine," I relented at last. "I promise." I didn't dare tell Colin, but it did provide me with some comfort to know he was looking out for me.

"And about last night…" Colin continued.

"Nope, you heard Paige and the rules." I laughed, happy to make sure he stuck to his promise, as well.

"Fine, but can we at least agree to put stuff behind us and be friends?" Colin asked, unable to let go of the tension in the room. I stared at him for a second. I couldn't fathom how he could look so good in sweats; it just didn't seem humanly possible.

"Sure, we can be friends, but that's all we are, got it?" I offered in a determined voice.

"Damn bro, she told you!" Christian bellowed, leaning forward and slugging his brother in the arm.

"Shut up, idiot," Colin barked, shoving his brother backward.

"How about both of you shut up and put the movie in!" Paige shouted.

"What are we watching?" I asked, wide-eyed, eager to ease the tension.

"*Scream* marathon!" Paige exclaimed, practically squealing in delight.

"You're kidding, right?" I moaned.

"Oh hell no, this girl never kids about her horror flicks," Christian advised me.

* * *

CHAPTER 13

The rhythm of the city had seemed to envelope me over the past couple of weeks. It almost felt like I had always been a part of its song. My routine began to bring me an immense comfort. I had managed to convert Paige to using a French press for our morning brew, rather than making a run past the coffee shop every day. I had also pieced together a decent wardrobe, thanks to a few trips with Paige to the thrift shops, Angel Street and Cure.

Where I came from, second hand shops were not somewhere you found what I would consider fashionable clothing. Angel Street and Cure had completely transformed my idea of a thrift store. Designer outfits were in the plenty, but the vintage pieces were the real find. It had become an invigorating challenge for me, or perhaps merely a distraction. Either way, I was hooked.

I had become accustomed over the past couple years to being haunted throughout my days by the memories of Ashton. Now, though, I had managed to drown out most of the painful thoughts, at least until the silent loneliness of the late night crept in. The familiar guilt always managed to find its way back to me just before I would drift off to sleep.

Ever since movie night at our place, Colin and I had found a comfortable place in our relationship. He had even taken to hanging out at the warehouse with me while I painted. I'd admit, at first it made me uncomfortable, but he had a way of making you warm up to him. Maybe it is just how damn sexy he was to look at, I didn't know. I think I never realized how funny he was until these past couple weeks. I told Paige the other night that I thought the guy would suffer through any amount of humiliation for a laugh.

The highlight for me had to be the night he was rummaging through salvage boxes from one of his renovation projects. It was over flowing with faux furs, pillbox hats, and what could only be described as a collection of your grandmother's jewelry. Before I knew what was happening, he was adorned from head to toe in the trinkets. If only I'd have had a pair of heels for him, I was certain he would have slipped them on for me. It took very little convincing to get him to agree to model for me, and it might be one of my favorite sketches of him.

Ever since Colin and I made our friendship truce, it had been just that, a real friendship. I was back on my path, focused on earning my degree, no longer consumed by distractions. Of course, I still thought Colin was insanely hot, and there were many times I had to remind my nether regions we were just friends, but now that I took the idea of a relationship off the table, things seemed to flow easier between us.

After weeks of nothing but work, Colin convinced me to agree to give him my Saturday. It wasn't a date or anything, despite how much Paige taunted me. He made it very clear, we would only be a couple of friends going out and having a good time. I had the hardest time falling asleep last night, anticipating what he might have planned for me today. I have never been able to handle surprises very well.

Glancing at the time on the screen of my iPhone, I began to fidget, checking to see if perhaps there was a text I had missed from Colin. It was not like him to be late, and even more unlike me to wait for someone when they were running late. *Fifteen minutes isn't the end of the world*, I told myself.

"Em!" Colin exclaimed, exiting the front door of his building. It usually drove me crazy when people would shorten my name to Em, I always thought of the letter 'M' when they would call me that. For some reason, though, it didn't bother me anymore when Colin did it.

"Um, hello? Really? I can't believe you would keep me waiting this long. I was about to give up on you," I complained, slapping him on the arm with the back of my hand.

"Totally my fault, you can be mad at me all you want," Colin offered with a smile, raising his hands in defense.

"Had trouble getting last night's flavor out of your bed?" I jested in a devilish tone.

"I wish that was the problem." Colin laughed.

I rolled my eyes in a mixture of amusement and

disgust. "So what was worth leaving me here, wasting my precious time?"

"Honestly? I had to toss Christian in the shower." Colin's voice changed, a solemnness suddenly taking over.

"Hmm ..." I began, furrowing my brow as I thought about the statement. "Isn't he a little too old to have his big brother taking care of bath time?"

"I know you and Paige are close, and I don't—well, I prefer she not know about this." Colin stared at me, as if waiting for me to confirm that I would keep his secret. I wanted to know, but at the same time, I felt incredibly uncomfortable about keeping anything from her. She had become my best friend, something I wasn't willing to betray.

"This just got a little too serious for me," I replied, shifting my hands in and out of my pockets uncomfortably.

"I know, and I shouldn't even be putting this on you, but I don't know who else to talk to," Colin pleaded. I could see the information he carried was quite a burden on him.

Shaking my head and holding up two open palms, as if to signal for him to stop, I advised, "All right, but a quick disclaimer: I won't keep a secret of infidelity or something like that from her."

"Christian would never do that—he loves Paige. He went out with some old buddies last night, and they got him drinking."

"Wait, isn't he in AA?" I asked, my concern obvious.

"Yup, he showed up this morning completely wasted. After about an hour of puking I managed to throw him in the shower. He's going to sleep it off and then hit a meeting as soon as he wakes up."

"I'm sorry." I reached out a hand and patted him on the arm, unsure what friend etiquette warranted.

"I worry about him; it's like he does this on purpose. As soon as things start going in the right direction for us, he has to go and do something stupid." I could see a different side of Colin as he spoke. He wasn't angry with his brother, it was clear he was concerned about him. There was no more joking around to cover up what he was going through.

"At least nothing terrible happened. It sounds like he knows he screwed up, and he is going to take care of things," I pointed out, trying to be the optimistic voice in the situation.

"We lost our parents when he was just a kid, and I know it was hard on him," Colin explained, unaware I had received the back-story of their entire life from Paige.

A silence lingered between us as Colin stared at the sidewalk, deep in thought. I wished I was one of those people who knew how to handle these situations. Instead, I just stood there, silent, like a complete idiot.

"You know what, we have a day full of fun to get to," Colin said, looking down at me. His face completely transformed in that moment. He went from intense and sad to chipper in only a few seconds—the transformation a bit unsettling at first. But quickly I remembered I was about to discover the surprise.

"Now, about this day of fun, you do realize that shoving dollar bills into strippers' G-strings is not my idea of a fun-filled day, right?" I asked, pressing my lips together to try and refrain from laughing.

"Damn, guess lunch at The Thunder From Down Under is out," Colin replied casually, starting to walk away from me.

"Oh wait," I squealed, leaping forward and grabbing his arm. "I take it back, I'm good with strippers."

"Nope, too late, I know how you really feel," Colin countered, taking my hand from his arm and wrapping it around his elbow so that we were walking, linked, side by side.

"Fine, no strip clubs, but can I have a hint about the rest of the day?" I begged, looking up at him, batting my eyelashes, as we moved down the sidewalk.

"You do realize that since you put the 'just friends' label on us, you have no power over me whatsoever with those eyes?" Colin taunted.

"Damn it!" I exclaimed.

Reaching the corner, Colin stepped one foot out into the street, and with an outstretched arm, he hailed a cab. Wherever he was taking me wasn't somewhere we could walk to. I was now even more intrigued.

"So you are seriously not even going to give me a hint?" I pressed, after a moment of silence in the cab.

"Let me see, I go through the trouble of writing the address down so that you won't hear me instructing the cabbie where to go, and you think I am now going to just tell you where we are going? Oh, my dear, you are a bit off your rocker, aren't you?" Colin stared at me in delight, thoroughly impressed with himself.

"You're loving this, aren't you?"

"Very much so."

I watched as the city passed by the window, one block, and then the next. Each time the cab would slow I crouched forward onto the front of my seat, but each time I was disappointed when he would again pick up speed. Silent, I held my breath, as we turned onto Madison, traveling farther uptown.

"Almost there," Colin finally remarked.

"We are?" I asked, looking around frantically, still completely unaware of where we might be going. The cab took a left onto 83rd Street, and as we came to a stop, before the next turn, I knew. Staring at me were the monstrous columns and stone facade that made up the front of the Metropolitan Museum of Art.

The cab proceeded to continue with another left onto 5th Avenue before pulling off to the curb. "Ready?" Colin asked pushing open the door and preparing to step out.

"The Met? Are you really taking me to The Met?" I asked, my jaw dropping as I stared at the front of the building that housed masterpieces from all across the world and throughout time.

"Well, I mean, only if you want to go." Colin stepped out, extending a hand.

"This is not a date," I reminded him after seeing how pleased he was with my reaction.

I stepped from the cab as he informed me, "I would never presume it was."

My heart began to race as we climbed the stone steps, nearing the entrance. I couldn't believe I had been in New York all of this time and not found the time to visit this landmark. I could feel Colin, watching me, living vicariously through my virgin experience.

I never realized how big the place was. I don't think Colin knew how to handle me once I was unleashed. It was three floors of bliss. In those halls there was no sadness, no tragic history to consume me. It was art; it was what I was born for. I raced through the American Wing, swooned over the Egyptian Art, slowly walked through, soaking up the Greek and Roman Art. All around me were the remnants of people who had lived long ago, people who expressed themselves in the same way I did. Their work spoke of their lives and their own personal tragedies. We grabbed lunch at a cafe before heading to the Modern Art area and then it was off to the Photography wing.

* * *

"Colin Bennett, you never cease to amaze me," I stated, leaning back in the cab with a gleeful sigh.

"It was my pleasure," he said, smiling.

"What are you doing for dinner?" I asked, not wanting the day to end.

"Ms. Hayes, are you asking me out on a date?" Colin laughed.

"No!" I exclaimed, pushing him playfully. "I simply would like to repay a friend for a wonderful day."

"I don't know? A guy could get the wrong idea."

"Oh my God!" I squealed as the cab came to a stop in front of my apartment. "You're relentless."

I watched as Colin's face twisted. He was staring out the window at something.

"Are you okay?" I asked, concerned by what might have him so perplexed.

Colin leaned forward, handing some cash to the cabbie through the opening in the plexi-glass. As he moved, I could suddenly see out the window behind him, and what he had been looking at. My heart sank as I realized William Stryker was waiting at my door.

"Crap," I whispered to myself.

"Do you want me to take care of this?" Colin offered, before opening the door.

I thought for a moment. I did want him to take care of it... I wanted him to make the creep leave me alone, but I knew that wouldn't be right. That wasn't the job of a friend.

"Nah, it's my problem. I'll get rid of him," I replied.

"I'm not leaving you alone with him. I don't care what you say," Colin insisted. I didn't dare tell him how happy that made me.

With a deep breath we exited the vehicle, and I waited as it drove away. Colin followed behind me, careful not to allow too much distance.

Stryker didn't wait for us to reach the door; instead, he rushed over to me the moment he saw us approaching.

"Clementine!" His voice made his agitation clear.

"Hello William," I answered coolly.

"Can we talk?" he asked looking over my shoulder at Colin.

"I'm not sure what we would have to talk about—"

"Alone," he added, as if it were a command.

"Not going to happen, buddy," Colin answered for me.

"So, this is why you haven't been returning my calls?" Stryker asked, shaking a hand wildly in Colin's direction.

"No, he's just a friend," I explained.

"Yeah, right." Stryker scoffed. "This is bullshit."

"It was one date, and I figured you would get the point I wasn't interested when I didn't talk to you for over a month," I snarled, deciding at last there was no delicate way to handle this madman. "Now, can you please leave me alone?"

"No, I won't. Not until I can talk to you alone," Stryker insisted.

"I already told you, it's not going to happen. Now please, do as the lady asked and don't bother her again. Come on, Em, let's get you upstairs," Colin said extending an arm and creating a barrier between Stryker and me.

"Don't you touch me!" Stryker shouted.

"Nobody is touching you, man. She just wants you to leave her alone," Colin quickly responded to his threatening gestures.

"I'll leave when I'm damn good and ready." Stryker was determined to have his say, even if I didn't want to hear it.

"What is it?" I growled.

"You and I have some business we need to discuss in private—stuff I'm sure you don't want pretty boy to hear," he spat angrily in my direction.

"Em, go inside," Colin interjected. I wasn't sure what to do. I didn't want to leave him to fight my battles, but I was also quickly becoming terrified of Stryker.

"Jesus, man, this isn't any of your damn business!" Stryker yelled in Colin's direction as I ran toward the security door, fumbling for the key.

"It is my business when you're harassing my friend. Now leave!" I had never seen Colin so aggressive, and no matter how close Stryker came to his face, he didn't move or shift his eyes.

Before I realized what was happening, the air exploded around us as Stryker reached back, landing a punch on Colin's right eye. The sound carried up and down the sidewalk as Colin's head gave way to the violent attack. Stryker wasted no time, using that opportunity to dart in my direction.

Colin, however, also didn't hesitate, and used the momentum to spin himself around and grabbed a hold of Stryker's waist, throwing him to the ground and pressing a knee into his chest. A couple swift punches later, and Colin rendered Stryker motionless.

Pushing Stryker deeper into the concrete, he stood and walked in my direction, motioning me to open the door. "Don't come back," Colin called over his shoulder.

In a moment we were inside my apartment, blood trickling down the side of Colin's face from the gash above his eye. I didn't know what to say... what could I say? Grabbing a washcloth from a drawer, I ran it under cold water and quickly brought it up to the wound. He winced as I applied pressure.

"I'm sorry," I whispered.

"Don't ever be sorry for the behavior of other people," Colin replied. If he only knew. I was always sorry for

what I drove other people to do. I had a knack for pushing
people over the edge.

CHAPTER 14

Three days had passed since the altercation between Stryker and Colin. William seemed to be successfully scared off, and apparently Colin had been too, since he hadn't called or shown up since. I had decided, however, this was for the best. It was clear Colin was becoming a distraction for me, even if I had been trying to convince myself he was not.

Today I received some exciting information, and the first person I thought of telling was Colin, which once more proved that some distance between us would be a good thing. Sliding my key into the apartment door, I turned the knob and waited a moment, listening for heavy breathing. Even though Paige had promised to control her and Christian's escapades, there seemed to be instances when they couldn't help themselves.

"Is that you, Emmie?" Paige called from the living room.

"Nah, just a robber here to steal your innocence," I yelled back, closing the door behind me and locking it.

"Too late, that was gone a long time ago." Paige laughed.

"Girl, you're not right," I remarked, walking past her into my room to drop my book bag on my bed. As I walked back into the living room I could instantly see that Paige had been crying. Rushing to her side, genuinely concerned, I asked, "What's wrong, sweetie?"

"Nothing," she quickly answered, looking away from me.

"Paige, your eyes are all red. Come on... something's wrong," I pushed, taking a hold of her hands and encouraging her to sit with me on the couch. "Is Christian all right?"

She sat, at last looking at me, clearly hesitant to talk about what was bothering her. I wanted more than anything for her to open up to me.

"You can talk to me," I pressed.

"I think he's lying to me," Paige said, her voice shaking, her eyes begging me to tell her she was wrong.

"What makes you think that?" I asked, keeping my voice quiet and calm.

"I don't know... a few nights ago he was out all night. I keep asking him what he was doing, but he's not being straight with me," Paige explained.

"Are you sure? I mean, how do you know he was lying?" I queried, remembering what Colin had told me about Christian's recent sobriety slip.

Paige pulled her sleeve down over her fingertips, using it to wipe a tear away before explaining, "At first he said he was home, and then when I told him I had stopped by his place and he wasn't there, he got nasty with me. He told I should stop checking up on him and asked why I can't just trust him. I never brought up trust—I only said I had stopped by and he wasn't there."

"That does seem odd." I had given my word to Colin, so what more could I say.

"He claims he must have just went out for a bite, but I know he's lying, Emmie. I don't know what to think. I never thought he was the type, but I think he might be cheating on me." As she spoke the words, it was as if a dagger was pressing into her heart. I was certain the truth would be better than the things that were running through her mind, but it wasn't my truth to tell.

"He's not cheating on you, sweetie," I comforted, squeezing her hand.

"How do you know? Why else would he lie to me?" she asked, staring up at me, hopeful.

"I just know Christian wouldn't do that. He loves you, hon. I'm sure whatever is going on is not as bad as you think." I reached out, giving her a hug, wishing more than anything I could tell her what I knew.

" I know you're probably right," she agreed. "I don't know what I should think, though; he has seemed so distant this week."

"Who knows, maybe he's going through something. You know how guys are… it's like pulling teeth sometimes." I offered the small amount of consoling I could.

"That's true, guys are idiots sometimes. Just look at Colin," Paige replied.

I stared at her, tilting my head, clearly puzzled by what she might be insinuating. "What's that supposed to mean?"

"Oh, come on, you have to know." Paige leaned back, pushing her head against the back of the sofa.

"Know what?" I asked, my heart starting to race.

"That he's totally hung up on you."

Paige's words made my breath catch in my throat. "What are you talking about? Colin is not hung up on me! He can't stand me; in fact, I haven't even seen him since he got in that fight with Stryker."

"Why do you think that is?" Paige inquired, not looking away from me.

"Because he realized being friends with me is more trouble than it's worth."

"Oh my God, you really are clueless, aren't you? You told him the two of you couldn't be anything more than friends, idiot. He told Christian he realizes he's falling for you, and he can't be around you if you don't want anything more."

"What? No—" In that moment it felt like a vice was tightening around my heart.

"Yes! He is head over heels for you, girl. How do you feel about him?" she asked, leaning forward, desperate for all the juicy details of my innermost thoughts.

"I don't know." I gasped, collapsing back onto the couch cushions.

"What don't you know? Colin is a great guy," Paige urged.

"He's a player."

"Emmie, give the guy half a chance, and I think he'll surprise you."

"I think I like him, too." I couldn't believe the words

that were coming out of my mouth. Did I seriously just say that I thought I might like him, too?

"Then go tell him!" She jumped to her feet, almost screaming in excitement.

I stood up, looking down at my skinny jeans and blouse. "I can't... I'm a mess."

"Oh, shut up, you look fine. He should be working on the loft with Christian." Paige practically shoved me out the door. "Come tell me what happens as soon as you talk to him, all right?"

"Okay, I will." My head was swimming. I grabbed my keys from the kitchen counter, not slowing down long enough to even think about what I was doing. If I did slow down long enough to think about it, I would probably chicken out.

"Oh my God! This is so freaking exciting!" Paige was no longer sad; instead, she was running in place, ready to explode.

"Wait, I almost forgot," I said halting and turning back to look at her.

"What?" She paused, holding her breath as she stared back at me.

"I'm a finalist for the gallery project. I have a real shot at a legit show."

"Flipping rock star! That's what you are, my friend." She pointed at me with a beaming smile. "Now go get that hottie."

It felt like my heart might explode out of my chest. Was this real? Did Colin actually tell Christian he had feelings for me? And even if he did tell him that, could I really have feelings for him, too? The thoughts were racing through my mind, question after question as I made my way down the sidewalk and into the loft.

As it came to a stop on Colin and Christian's floor, I thought for a moment I might vomit. Bracing myself against the wall with one arm, I swallowed deeply and knocked on the door.

"Come in," I heard Christian's voice from the other side of the door. How was I going to do this? Was I going to talk to Colin right in front of his brother? What the hell was I going to say? I wasn't actually doing this, was I? Yup, here I go. My hand was really opening the door. One step and then another, and I was inside their living room.

Looking to the right I immediately saw Christian—he was pulling down the upper, mismatched kitchen cabinets. Pausing and glancing over at me, he gave a half smile, "Oh, hey Emmie, what's up?"

I stood there, not knowing what to say at first as he continued his work. Maybe I should blurt out, I think your brother is amazing, and I heard he might like me, too, so where is that gorgeous piece of ass? But no, that didn't seem right at all. "Is Colin around?"

"Nope, not sure where he went or when he'll be back," Christian replied without looking at me.

"Okay, thanks." And that was it; I turned around and walked out, with no explanation. What was I thinking? Colin not being there was for the best. I had told myself more times than I cared to count that I was here for art school, not to find some boyfriend. It was quite obvious I wasn't cut out for love, and I didn't know how many more ways the world could tell me that fact.

Closing the door to the lift, I decided the best thing for

me at this point would be to take my mind off Colin and all the confusing thoughts racing through my mind about him. Pressing the button to take me up another floor, I tried my best to focus my thoughts on the gallery project, reminding myself that was why I was in New York in the first place.

The lift ground to a halt, causing me to stagger slightly. Pulling up the gate I sighed as I stared at the canvas across the room. The burgundy swirled as it mixed with the teal, looking almost liquid, the white that tickled at the edges exploded into what looked like little bits of foam, reminding me of the ocean. I loved the way my paintings made me feel. That's enough. Who needs love?

As I walked closer to my painting I gasped when I saw the back of Colin's head. He was standing at the window, peering out at the street. I loved the way he made me feel. Just a glimpse of him made my heart flip and created an ache between my legs. Why was he here? I was beginning to resign myself to the idea of not telling him about the feelings I had for him, and then he shows up.

"Colin?" I whispered softly as I approached.

When he turned to look at me I felt my stomach drop, the skin around his eye had turned into a dance of blues and purples with a yellowish hue licking at the edges of the bruise. My jaw fell open in shock.

"It looks that good, huh?" he asked, delivering a half smile.

"Oh my God! I'm so sorry that happened to you."

"I told you, don't ever apologize for what assholes do."

"I never got a chance to thank you," I said taking a few steps closer.

"You don't have to thank me; anyone else would have done the same thing."

"Somehow I doubt that."

"Has he left you alone?" Colin asked, studying me.

"I haven't heard anything from him," I replied truthfully.

"Good. That's good. I should have checked in sooner. I'm sorry, I was… I don't know what I was—"

"Please, don't worry about it." The space between us was now only mere inches. He smelled like fresh wood shavings. "I just hope you're not mad at me."

Colin's eyebrows pressed together, a troubled look consuming his face. "Do you really think I could be mad at you for that?"

"I don't know, I guess. I'm feeling like trouble kind of follows me." I laughed lightly, trying to lift the somber mood. Sensing my attempt, Colin smiled. "Oh! I got some fantastic news today!"

"Oh yeah?" Colin inquired, tilting his head, still staring at me with great intensity. I could feel his eyes burning into me.

"I found out I'm a finalist in the gallery project." Actually saying it out loud, I hoped it didn't come across as bragging.

"That's amazing!" Colin exclaimed, throwing his arms around me, lifting me off the ground into an embrace. In an instant, I felt like I was soaring, pulling my feet up behind me. As he set me back on the ground, our eyes locked, and I wished the moment would never end. I didn't want him to pull away, and based on his lingering grasp, he didn't either.

But it did end. Colin took an uncomfortable step back, shaking his head. "I'm sorry, I shouldn't—"

"It's okay," I interrupted.

"No, it's not okay, Em. It's not okay because I can't do this."

"I don't understand... do what?"

Colin turned and looked back out the window. "I know something bad happened to you. Some horrible thing in your past that you don't talk about."

"How do you—" the words stuck in my throat.

"Anyone who gets to know you can tell you have walls, and there's only one reason to build walls. Look, I get that, and if you don't want to talk about it, that's your choice. What I can't do is pretend that I just want to be your friend. I can't be close to you and not want to kiss you. I can't see the way you light up when you experience things for the first time and not want to hold you."

My mind was spinning. Was I dreaming this entire interaction? No, he was real, and my next words came out as a whisper, "I don't know what to say."

"There's nothing to say. I came here to tell you that I couldn't make these feelings go away. I respect you, and I understand you're not interested in anything more than a friendship, but I can't pretend, so I can't be around you anymore. If I'm around you, I don't think I'll be able to control myself," he said, turning back to face me, his gray eyes staring all the way into my soul.

"Colin, please don't."

"This was hard enough for me to say, so don't make it any—" he started, but I cut his words off, lifting up onto my toes, my chest pressing against him as my lips met his.

My head was spinning, no questions, no thoughts besides what I wanted in that moment. I wanted *him*.

Colin wasted no time, wrapping his arms around me and pulling me even closer to his body. He thrust his tongue outward, parting my lips with ease. All I could think about was his touch. I hadn't allowed myself to even admit it, but I had been longing for it since we met. I closed my eyes, the moment enveloping me.

When the kiss came to an end, I looked into his gaze; he was still holding me close. "What does this mean?" he asked softly.

"I don't know," I replied honestly, my heart pounding.

"What do you want this to mean?"

I shook my head, "I don't know."

"Do you want me?" he questioned.

I paused, scared to answer, but even more frightened not to. I didn't want it to end. I wanted his hands and lips to explore every inch of my body and at the same time I was terrified. I nodded, and his eyes widened in delight.

A chill rushed down my spine as I felt his breath on my cheek. He gazed at me; I licked my lips slowly in anticipation, running my fingers down his back until they met the bottom of his t-shirt. I pulled slightly upward, and he took the hint. Releasing me, he lifted the shirt above his head, allowing it to drop to the floor, exposing his bare chest and chiseled stomach.

I smiled, biting my lip as I drank him in. He was more than anything I had imagined. Colin stepped forward, taking hold of my shirt and releasing the buttons, one by one. When my blouse finally fell open, exposing my overflowing bra and slight tummy I felt my face grow hot. I wasn't fat, I knew that, but I also wasn't fit like him.

My eyes shifted to the ground as my insecurities overwhelmed me. A man hadn't seen me naked in years, and now, here I was, standing with all my vulnerabilities exposed, in front of this Greek god-like specimen, with nothing for me to hide behind.

My hands slid in front of me to hide my tummy but just as quickly he grabbed my wrists and pulled them to my side. "My God, you're beautiful," he whispered.

I shook my head, denial of his words consumed me. He released my wrists and reached up, lifting my chin so our eyes would meet once again. There, in that moment, I saw it. I saw truth. I saw who I was through his eyes, and I was beautiful.

My heart literally skipped a beat as I allowed my shirt to drop to the floor. We both feverishly tugged at our pants, as if we were in a competition to see who could remove them first.

I stood there, in just my bra and panties, suddenly more confident than I had ever been, thanks to the way he looked at me. Colin stood there, his black boxer briefs hugging him perfectly, revealing the outline of his erection.

He stepped closer, the space between us now barely existent. I could hear him breathing, see his chest moving in and out. Opening my hand, I placed my palm against his chest, and though the warehouse was drafty, he was warm to the touch. I felt myself get more turned on with each passing beat of his heart.

"Damn it, Em," he moaned.

"What?" I asked looking up at him, fearful I had already done something wrong.

"I was fine with the way my life was. Now you're all I can think about." He sighed, "I think I'm falling in love with you."

I couldn't tell if the ache in my chest was from joy or from my heart breaking. I swore I wasn't ever going to fall in love again. It hurt too much. *Don't think about it*, I told myself, *just kiss him*.

Pressing up onto my tiptoes again, I met his lips with mine, our tongues quickly finding one another.

He pressed his erection against my hip, slipping his hands behind my back to unclasp my bra. I tried not to think about what an expert he was with his technique. It would only serve to aggravate me.

Our bodies separated for a moment, but keeping our necks arched, we managed to continue kissing as he relieved me of my bra. My D-cup breasts falling into their natural position, he once again pressed against me, lifting a finger to one of my breasts and traced my exposed nipple.

He kissed his way down my throat, taking the hand away from my breasts and slipping it behind my neck, allowing my head to fall back, enjoying the exploration of his lips.

He pushed even harder against me, causing me to stumble back several steps, until my calves hit the couch, and I realized it was intentional. He guided my body, laying me down onto the sofa. Looking down at me, Colin smiled, and in that moment I thought that in itself might be enough to make me orgasm. Bending over, he made quick work of slipping off my panties. For a fleeting moment I wished I had worn a cuter pair, but then he was on top of me and all other thoughts were gone.

He kissed his way down my body, tracing my belly button with his tongue. When I realized where he was headed I quickly stiffened and began to struggle. He paused, shaking his head no, then looked up at me with a devilish stare.

"Please," was all he said, and I relented, relaxing against him.

His tongue found my clit without much effort, flicking wildly against it. My back arched as the wetness overcame me as an ache I had forgotten even existed began to grow inside of me.

"Oh God," my back stiffened as he whispered into my folds. "I want you so bad."

I was more than prepared to give him what he wanted and without thinking I reached down and pulled on one of his arms. He took the hint and climbed back on top of me, parting my legs even wider with his body.

I tugged at the waistband of his boxer-briefs, and he gladly assisted me with the removal. I giggled at the urgency with which he did so, catching a glimpse of him momentarily blushing.

I needed him to know I wanted him just as much. Wrapping my hand around his girth, I moaned in delight. He smiled, pressing against me, causing me to release him and wrap my arms and legs around his torso.

With a thrust he entered me. My skin began to burn, as his lips grazed my cheek, his breathing growing heavier. He pushed himself up onto his knees, still inside me. I looked up at him, and his eyes locked onto mine just before his mouth found my breasts again. I exhaled. As I pushed the air out of me, a muscle deep within began to twitch against him.

One of my hands slipped down to the side of the couch, gripping the fabric tightly. He took his time.

"Does that feel good?" he whispered with a grin on his face.

Unable to create a recognizable response, I whimpered. My legs stiffened each time he pulled away as they tried to keep him close. I began to convulse, losing control of my body. Lifting his lips up to mine, he kissed me, and I melted into him, no longer able to hold myself together, his mouth absorbing my cries.

Sliding one hand beneath me and running it to my lower back, he lifted me into him with each motion. I could tell from his gaze he could see the climax building within me. He wanted the release, that was clear, but more so, he wanted to feel mine. The moment my muscles within began to spasm, giving way to the climax, I saw his jaw clench and my lip quivered as we found the moment of release together. After only a couple pulses, his lips found mine again. I whimpered, overwhelmed as he kissed me deeply. He tasted of satisfaction.

CHAPTER 15

*S*taring into the bathroom mirror, the fluorescent light flickering above my head, I used my hands to cup water, splashing my face. I pulled my frizzy mess of hair into a loose and high ponytail. I was starting to see my age in the reflection that stared back at me, small lines tickling the corners of my eyes. It could also be the fact that I barely got any sleep last night. Every time I tried to separate myself from Colin he would pull me back into him for another romp.

I wasn't complaining. Mind you I had forgotten I could feel those things, and what a glorious reminder it was. I was still wearing the same clothes as the previous night. Once the morning light had begun to shine in through the windows, I had decided it was best not to return to the apartment. I knew if Paige heard me she would never release me without a full report of all the details.

Quite honestly, at this point I wouldn't even know what to tell her. Colin and I dozed off into each other's arms when the exhaustion finally overcame us. I awoke before him and thought I would sneak out unnoticed, but, much to my dismay, he was a light sleeper. Although, I can't really blame him, considering we were wrapped around one another on the sofa.

He wanted to talk about everything the second we were awake, which of course was the last thing I wanted to do. I tried to end things in a way that wouldn't make it awkward between us. I told him what a wonderful time I had and hoped maybe we could do it again, but that only seemed to agitate him.

He wanted to talk about a possible relationship. The more he talked, the more it felt like all of the oxygen was being sucked out of the room. I managed to give an excuse about having a full day and I would talk to him after I got home, which I had no intention of doing.

Digging through my bag, I pulled out my facial powder, blush, and mascara. My mom always told me they were the only three things a woman with natural beauty needed. I missed her. I had tied my blouse in a knot off to one side in an effort to make the outfit I was wearing fresh, in case any classmates might have noticed the re-wear. I now knew it was naive of me to think that any of them even noticed I was in the same class.

Slipping my make-up back into my bag, I sighed. *Not too bad*, I thought. If the Chatty Kathy routine this morning was any indicator, Colin would most certainly be waiting for me to get home. I had already devised a plan to walk a block out of my way and come up the street past the warehouse. That way, unless he was waiting for me at my place, I would successfully avoid him.

Bounding down the stairs and out the front door of the school, I squinted as the sun temporarily stole my vision. Fumbling for my sunglasses, I paused a moment until they were securely in place upon the bridge of my nose. The breeze blew against my face, causing a few loose strands of hair to pull away from the collective group and dance in the wind.

"Hey beautiful," Colin said in a soft yet deep voice. My heart first swelled, quickened in pace, and then sank, as if I were on a roller coaster.

I spun around, taking several steps toward him, an invisible force drawing me near. I was smiling. *Why are you smiling?* I didn't have an answer for myself, at least not one I was willing to admit.

"Colin, what are you doing here?" I asked, falling into his grasp. *What are you doing? Don't fall into his arms; you need to resist his charms.* No matter what I told myself, in that moment, I was unable to resist his charms.

He pressed his lips against my forehead, and a chill ran down my spine. "Are you kidding me? I tried to sleep, and when that didn't work, I tried to get some work done. I gave up on that around lunchtime and decided I would come and wait for you. Can I walk you home?"

"Of course," I replied, taking a position next to him and locking my arm around his, thankful I had taken the time to spruce myself up moments ago. I don't know how he did it, but when I was away from him I could think clearly, where I was free from his captivating gaze. The moment he came near me, though, his intoxicating smell that made me think of a rugged lumber jack, shirtless in the woods, his sparkling eyes that made me dizzy, combined to turn me into a pile of goo.

We proceeded to walk down the sidewalk; I could feel the eyes of all the ladies we walked past, staring at me, wishing they could take my place. Damn, why did that feel so good?

"Well, I was hoping that perhaps you had time to think about what we talked about this morning," Colin said. I could feel his eyes on me.

"It was a busy day," I lied. The only thing I had been thinking about since I left his side was what we had talked about. I didn't want him to know that my head was telling me to run away from him as fast as I could before someone got hurt, while everything in my body was screaming at me to go for it. Though I tried to look at things logically, and justify my reaction to him as a simple case of lust, when I was with him I couldn't resist.

"Em, I know what you think about me, but I'm more than that," Colin explained.

"Oh yeah, and just what makes you think you know what I think of you, Mr. Bennett?" *I* wasn't even sure what I thought of Colin anymore. I was certain I enjoyed being around him, but even more certain anything between us would only end badly.

"Let's just say a little bird told me." Colin grinned.

"Paige," I growled, realizing he was referring to my comments about him being a player, which I thought had been made in confidence.

"I'm not going to lie to you. I'll never lie to you. I have been with a lot of women in my life."

"Yeah, I kind of gathered that between Paige's ex-roommate and the bimbo at the bar who had her tongue down your throat."

"I thought that was against the rules to talk about?" Colin asked with a grin.

"Oh, you can't talk about it, but I can say whatever I want about it."

He laughed. "Is that right?"

"Yup, those are the rules. You agreed to them—nothing we can do about it now."

"I see. I'm going to be so honest with you, even though I think that I may destroy any chance I might possibly have of getting you to date me."

"That juicy? Do go on," I prodded.

"I'm not sure what Paige told you about my past, but I think you need to know more about who I am. I pretty much raised Christian. All I've ever wanted is for him to have a happy life. Filling our parents' shoes wasn't easy, and I always thought it meant love wasn't an option for me. I thought I had too many responsibilities. If it meant Christian had a chance at being happy, I was willing to give up my own happiness." Colin's tone became extremely serious as he went on to discuss his wild past.

"And how do you think all of those women felt about being used like that?" I questioned, remembering the pain on Bailey's face.

"I know it doesn't seem like much, but if I ever hurt any of those women, it was not intentional. I have always been upfront that I wasn't looking for love. Some of them thought they could change me, make me into the guy they wanted me to be."

"And why exactly should I put myself through that?" I asked, avoiding his glare, keeping my eyes focused on the path in front of us.

"I've never felt anything like this, Em. I'm not looking for just sex. I want to be with you, and I want you to only be with me." Colin sounded hurt that I could even ask the question.

What did he mean he had never felt like this? Things are getting far too serious already. You need to end this while you still can, I told myself.

"Nothing has changed for you—Christian is still your number one priority." There wasn't anything he could say to dispute that; anyone could see Christian was the driving force in his life.

"He was. But now someone else has become a priority to me."

Damn it.

I stopped, unable to move. I pulled my arm from his and backed against the brick wall, needing it to steady myself. "Don't say stuff like that. Your brother is your life, and I'm just some girl."

He moved in close to me, pressing against my body, lifting my chin with his fingertips, and forcing me to look into his eyes. "You're not just *some* girl. Why do you think he ended up getting wasted the other night? I'm so distracted, all I can think about is you."

"Great, now you're saying it's my fault your brother fell off the wagon!" I exclaimed, attempting unsuccessfully to break away.

"No! Damn it, Em, why do you have to make things so hard? I'm just trying to say I love my brother, and that will never change, but I have put him first long enough. I want more in my life now. I want you." I did make things hard, impossible in fact, so why couldn't he see how much misery I was going to bring him—how much pain we would bring to each other.

"You don't mean that," I argued. I wanted to tell him who I really was, what I was capable of, but it was a secret I had sworn never to reveal.

"Why would you say that? Don't you think I'm man enough to decide what I want?" he demanded, his hands shaking in frustration.

He needed to know that I was no good for him; he needed to know I left a path of destruction behind me. I looked directly into his eyes, refusing to allow the pools of gray to swallow me in their depths. "Colin, I'm broken. I don't want to be with you because if I was, you would end up just as broken as me."

"That's bull. It's an excuse. We all have pasts, but nothing is so bad we can't overcome it."

"You don't know that." Why was he being so relentless? I needed him to let it go, but he just kept pushing.

"So tell me," Colin pleaded.

I didn't move. I didn't breathe. I wanted to tell him. I wanted to give it all over to him with the hope he could take the pain and make it go away. But I couldn't. I would keep drowning the sorrow deep within.

"I can't," I finally whispered. *Run. Just turn and run away from him right now. You are not strong enough for this yet.* I tried to do what my mind was pleading for me to do, but instead I found myself standing there, waiting for him to give me a reason—a reason for me to stop running, to stop hurting all the time.

"Fine, don't tell me. But don't do this—don't push me away. Let me love you." Love me? He didn't know the things I knew about love. It was a beast that chewed you up and spit you out.

"I can't hurt you, too," I whispered.

"Who else have you hurt, sweetie?" Colin asked. I knew he saw the wave of sadness consume me. I couldn't answer; the pain of my past was too great. Reaching his arms out, he pulled me into his protective cocoon. "I see you, baby, all of you, so please, let me at least try."

What are you doing? You know what happened with Ashton—you use people up until there is nothing left of them. Don't do that to Colin. The more I scolded myself internally, the more I started to think maybe I needed Colin. Maybe I was so broken I couldn't be put back together without someone's help. *That's a dangerous gamble... are you willing to gamble Colin's heart on that? Think about the last man's heart you broke.*

"I don't know," I said at last.

"I'm not asking for you to commit the rest of your life to me, Em," Colin explained. "All I want is for you to give us a chance. If I can't make you happy, then I will understand."

I dug my fingers deeper into his body, before confessing, "I'm scared."

"This is scary stuff." He didn't ask me why, or of what. He accepted my fear. I loved that.

"What if we hurt each other?" I asked, positive he couldn't have a good answer for me.

Colin considered my question before taking a step back to look at me. His hands slid down my arms, taking hold of my wrists. He bent slightly, forcing me to look him in the eyes. "That's a chance I'm willing to take. I think what we could have together is worth so much more than the risks. Please, don't give up on us before we even get started."

This is where you say no, I thought. But that didn't happen. Instead I nodded. I couldn't believe I was agreeing. Everything I promised myself I would never do again, and here I was, departing from the reality I had accepted and losing all control. He made me feel again—my heart ached, and he consumed me in a way I never thought possible. Terrified, I kept nodding yes… yes to a chance. I only hoped neither of us would regret it.

CHAPTER 16

"*N*o seriously, I want to know," Paige insisted, following me from room to room as I tried to escape her incessant questioning.

"You're funny, but now will you please drop it?" I begged.

"Not until you tell me if he cries when he climaxes." Paige's statement practically made her squeal with delight.

"Oh my God, babe! Please, no more!" Christian yelled from the couch. "Isn't it bad enough he actually forbade me from going back to the loft tonight?"

I stopped dead in my tracks; I could still hear Paige snickering from behind me. Walking to the open doorway of my bedroom, I stared intensely at Christian as I asked, "Why would you not be allowed to go back to the loft?"

"He didn't say exactly, but it's not something I really want to give too much thought to, if you know what I mean," he snarled, not pleased with being kicked out for the evening.

"I bet I know why…" Paige taunted gleefully.

"Will you stop already?" I groaned, running into my bedroom and slipping a pair of canvas flats on.

"Oh, come on, just a little more," she whined, swinging halfway into my room, hanging from the doorframe. "Are we talking Vienna sausage or foot long?"

"Gross!" Christian shouted, skillfully tossing a throw pillow, and nailing Paige in the back of the head.

"Whatever, I need to go," I replied, pushing past her, giving a quick disapproving roll of my eyes.

"Wait, that's what you're wearing?" she asked.

Looking down at my jeans and tight fitting t-shirt I smiled, "Yup."

"No, he's planning a romantic night, so you need to wear something sexy," Paige argued.

"I am," I insisted, walking to the front door and opening it.

"That is not sexy!" Paige yelled back.

"You haven't seen what I'm wearing under it," I replied, barely able to contain my laughter. I wished in that moment her face had been visible to me, I am certain her expression would be priceless.

"Oh, you slut!" she cried.

As I pulled the door closed behind me, I heard Christian moaning in disgust. I made my way to Colin's place, and by that time, my imagination was running wild as to what he might have planned for the evening. We had been dating for a couple weeks now, and the world had not spun off its axis, a tsunami had not hit the city, and best of all, Colin did not press me about my past. All winners in my book.

The lift stopped, and I raised the door, trying to

convince the butterflies in my stomach to stop battling. I thought after you dated someone for a little while these feelings were supposed to cease, but apparently I had not reached that threshold with Colin. Every time I was about to meet up with him, the same feelings would rise in me. It didn't help that when I walked into a room he would give me a look like he wanted to strip me naked with his teeth.

Another thing I hadn't figured out: when did you stop knocking on the door? I mean if you were an exclusive item, did you have to knock every time you walked into the other person's place? He had a key to my apartment since he was our landlord, but he had never actually used it without permission after we made the commitment to exclusively see one another.

Clearing my throat, I reached out my newly polished fingertips and repeatedly tapped my knuckles on the door.

"Em?" I heard his muffled voice yelling from a distant room.

"Yeah, it's me," I called back, feeling a little goofy yelling through the door.

"Come on in."

I tried the door, but much to my dismay it did not open. "It's locked."

Pressing my cheek against the cool steel, I heard his footsteps bounding toward me. A moment later there was some clicking and sliding noises, the door finally pulling open to reveal his smiling face. Damn, he was sexy. "We're going to have to get you a key made."

I guess that answered that question. I followed him

into the main room, pausing as he closed and locked the door behind me. The recent push he and Christian had made to get the drywall hung, had made all the difference since I had last seen the space. It was starting to actually resemble a home rather than a squatter's paradise.

"Oh, babe, it's looking so good in here," I offered, my eyes shifting to the kitchen, where the new dark upper cabinets were now completely hung.

Colin laughed at my response. "Not such a rat hole anymore, huh?"

"You're never going to let me live that down, are you?" I asked, lifting my eyebrows.

"Eventually… maybe," he teased. "It's got a long way to go out here, but this wasn't why I wanted you to come over here tonight."

I turned toward him, reaching out with my free hand to grab his, pulling him closer and pressing my body against him. "Oh yeah? And just why exactly did you bring me here?"

Running his nose along mine, he brought it to rest just above my lips. "Slow down, girl, we have plenty of time for that."

My face flushed as the embarrassment washed over me. Had we actually reached a point where I was starting to over-sex him? "I'm sorry, I thought you wanted—"

His lips pressed against mine, stealing my words away. When he pulled back, he looked into my eyes. "Oh, I definitely want that, but this night is all about you. Let's take our time."

"I like the sound of that," I muttered.

Pulling away, he turned and walked toward the master

bedroom, pausing just outside and staring at me, beck-oning me with his eyes to join him.

"Wait, I thought we weren't going to do that right now," I playfully jested, not budging from where I stood.

"I have a surprise for you—now will you get over here," he said, more as a command than a question.

"A surprise?" I asked, allowing him to take my hand as I approached.

"Yes, close your eyes."

I gave him a disapproving glare. "This isn't going to end well for me, is it?"

Colin smiled. "Will you just close your eyes?"

Pursing my lips together, I reluctantly obeyed. I heard the door to the master bedroom open, and he guided me through the doorway.

"Turn a little this way," he instructed. "Okay, open."

When the darkness fell away, an amazing scene was revealed. Since I met the Bennett brothers, I had been forced to use the guest bathroom in the main part of their living quarters. The construction efforts in the master bath, which had been kept under wraps and handled exclusively by Colin, were off limits to anyone else. The only way to describe what I was looking at: an absolute masterpiece. The room had become a work of art.

My head turned from side to side, wildly, as I tried to take everything in. Though an enchanting chandelier hung over the oval-shaped bathtub, the room was lit by the dozens of candles that littered the floor and counter of an old buffet, which had been restored and converted into a double vanity. Two of the walls, from floor to ceil-ing, were covered in small, one-inch tiles that reflected as if they were made of pearls. At the far end there was a stand up shower stall, entirely encased in glass, an over-sized shower-head hanging in the center, ready to create a waterfall for its inhabitant.

In the corner, across from the shower, was a door, which I assumed, led to the toilet. Perhaps the tray of delectable looking goodies should have been what surprised me the most, but it wasn't. What took my breath away was when I caught site of a painting near the bathtub. It was one of mine—I remember naming it black tears. It was of a young girl, her head hanging low, her eyes closed, a darkness all around her, and as her mascara ran down her cheeks they created the trails of black tears.

"How?" I gasped in disbelief.

"Your mother," he answered with a huge grin.

"What?" I looked at him, completely confused.

"I thought the email contact form on your website would go to you. I might have typed some inappropriate things, and your mother was quick to set me straight on how one treats a lady with respect."

"Oh God, you didn't?" I stared at him, horrified.

"It's okay. After I got the severe tongue lashing, I explained who I was. She said she was handling all of the shipping of your back stock while you were away at school," Colin explained, but all I could think about was the fact that he had talked to my mother and apparently said some dirty things. I wasn't sure I would ever be able to speak to her again.

"Who did you tell her you were?" I pushed.

"Don't worry, I didn't use the word *boyfriend*. I told her I liked her daughter a lot, and I would like to get even closer to her." Colin gave me a very pointed stare as he told me how the conversation went.

"I'm sorry, I didn't mean it like that. I told her I was starting to see someone, so it's not like you're a complete secret."

"I know," Colin said, a smile plastered across his face. He walked over and picked up a strawberry from the tray waiting on the vanity.

"How do you know that?"

"She told me."

"Oh, she did, huh? And what exactly did she tell you?" I inquired, not taking my eyes off him as he turned and lifted the ripe fruit to my lips. I took a bite, the juice running down my chin.

"That you said I'm hot." He didn't wait for me to rebut, kissing the liquid off my chin, traveling down my neck.

"I can't think straight when you do that," I whispered, my eyes closing.

"I know." He seemed to know a lot of things.

I stood there, waiting for more, but a moment passed and I realized he was gone. Opening my eyes I saw he was bent over the oval tub. Silent, I watched as he turned on the water, carefully checking the temperature. He then plugged it up and walked over to retrieve a bottle from the vanity.

"What are you doing?" I asked in the most flirtatious voice I could manage. I always worried I sounded juvenile when I tried to use my cute and sexy voice.

"I told you, tonight is all about you. Now take your clothes off," he demanded, pouring a small amount of blue liquid into the water. I didn't move, rather just watched as the liquid began to froth and foam into a bubbly mass, steam filling the air around us. He turned to face me, lifting a single eyebrow, delivering the sinister gaze that always caused me to quiver. "Come on, or do you need me to come over there and undress you?"

"Wait, what about dinner? I mean, I thought we were going to get dinner," I stammered, barely able to keep standing from the prospect of getting naked with him in a bathtub.

Colin placed the bottle in his hands at his feet, and then approached me slowly. "I made some appetizers for you to enjoy in the bath, and dinner is in the oven. Do you want to eat, or do you want to be pampered?"

"You made dinner?" I questioned, my skeptical glare revealing all of my doubts.

"Believe it or not, I'm quite capable when I put my mind to things." He smiled, and I had to stop myself from attacking him.

I didn't need to give it another moment's thought; I knew I was ready for this pampering. I quickly unbuttoned my pants, using my feet and legs to shimmy them down, flicking them off violently from the final foot they clung to. Colin was now directly in front of me, barely any space between us, and his eyes told me he was pleased with my sudden enthusiasm. Before I could lift my shirt, he had his hands grasped tightly around it, pulling it over my head.

"Holy hell," he growled, as my black lacy bra and panty set came into complete view. My stomach fluttered, and an ache grew inside me as I saw his response. "You'll have to wear these for me again."

Grabbing my hips, he spun me around, pulling my backside against his pelvis. Based on the hardness grinding against my hip, I could tell he was more pleased with my outfit than I originally assumed. Slipping his hands beneath my underwear, at my hips, he guided them along my legs, creating a trail of kisses down my back as he went, nibbling softly on my bare ass cheek for a brief second.

Standing back up, he swept my hair over one shoulder and unclasped my bra. I allowed it to fall to the floor, turning to face him. Taking one hand, he led me to the bath, guiding me into the awaiting suds. The warm water swallowed me, finding its way into all of my crevices. Twisting the handles, stopping the flow of water, he stared.

"Aren't you going to join me?" I asked, saddened by his fully clothed body.

"Patience, my love."

I watched him longingly as he retrieved the tray of treats, placing it on the floor near us. Glancing over the edge of the tub I took a quick inventory: strawberries, grapes, chocolate pieces, small squares of cheese, baguette slices topped with freshly cut tomatoes. When my eyes shifted up to him, he surprised me with an extended hand, his fingers offering me a glass of red wine.

"You are too much," I commented, taking it from him and sipping the vintage, appreciating the earthiness of it.

"Never too much," he replied, flipping through his iPhone.

"Okay, I've been patient, now you get naked," I stated firmly.

"Jesus, girl, what did we awaken in you?" Colin laughed, not shifting his eyes from the screen.

"Get in here, and I'll show you—" Just as I finished my sentence, from hidden places within the ceiling came a sweet melody by La Roux, and I shouted. "Get out!"

"Right? I wired it before I even did the drywall," he boasted proudly.

"You have officially blown my mind."

"Not yet, but I will," he muttered under his breath, the childish sexual innuendo making me smile.

Once the music was playing he wasted no time relieving himself of his clothes. I began to throw catcalls in his direction, which he was happy to oblige me with an extremely sexy sway of his hips. With only his boxers on, he looked at me, waiting for me to let him know just how bad I wanted the full monty.

"Come on, baby, show me what you got," I quipped playfully. And then he did. I reached a hand out toward him, but he pulled away, shaking a finger at me, as if I was being naughty.

"We have all night," Colin informed me as he walked around to the side of the tub opposite of me and slid in.

"And what exactly do you have planned for this all-night marathon?" I inquired, watching him sink into the clouds of white, his legs grazing mine.

"Hmm... I want to leave some things as a surprise, but how long has it been since you've had a massage with real massage oils?"

"Good question... let's see," I responded, pretending to try and remember. "Oh yeah, never."

"Then I'm glad I get to pop that cherry."

"You're going to be my undoing, Colin Bennett."

"I hope so; it's only fair since you were mine," he said, beckoning me closer. I turned, sliding my back against his still semi-hardness, laying my head against his chest, his arm wrapping around me, his fingertips coming to rest just below my breasts. Expelling all the air from my lungs I closed my eyes, soaking in the peacefulness of the moment. No more pain haunting every thought, the guilt had found another place to live... at least for now. The only thing that plagued me these days was an over-whelming desire to be right here, in his arms.

CHAPTER 17

ou can do this. You open your mouth, and you just tell him. You know you need to do this—it's not right to keep moving forward and not tell him. I told myself this as I stared in my bathroom mirror. The closer Colin and I had been growing, the more I felt like I should be telling him about Ashton and my past.

He shared so many intimate details with me, about when his parents died, or when his uncle basically abandoned them. There was even the night where he was almost in tears, telling me what a failure he felt like when Christian lost control of his sobriety. I sat there listening, nodding, consoling, but when he looked to me to reciprocate the giving, I simply sat there with a blank stare on my face.

He never pushed me, but I could tell he knew there was something behind my wall that I didn't want him knowing. I could see that it was hurting him, and the last thing I wanted to do was hurt Colin.

"Emmie, Colin's here," Paige called from the other room.

I looked in the mirror one last time. Tonight, tell him tonight.

Emerging from my room I could feel all eyes on me. "What?" I asked, looking down at my most recent thrift store find—a mini dress with a sequined silver top.

"You look hot," Paige said, her mouth hanging open.

"Thanks," I replied beaming a smile back.

"I concur," Colin added coming up behind me and wrapping an arm around my waist.

"Pace yourself, guys," Christian snapped from the edge of the kitchen.

"Oh, come on, I've been watching you and Paige going at it for years." Colin laughed at his brother's reaction.

"That's different," Christian argued, unable to support his claim with any facts.

"Yeah, whatever you say. Grab your coats, ladies; we don't want to be late," Colin instructed.

For the first time, I stopped and took a good, long look at Colin. He was wearing distressed jeans and a red and blue button up plaid flannel shirt. "Wait, am I over dressed?" I asked, suddenly feeling very uncomfortable.

"No way," Colin replied.

"I thought we were going to a concert," I said, searching for details.

"We are," Colin answered plainly.

"Where at?" I questioned, not trusting his assurance that my attire was appropriate.

"Half Kings," Christian answered as Colin's eyes shot daggers.

"What? Oh my God, I'm changing. I'm way over dressed," I complained.

"No!" Colin exclaimed. "I'm not letting you take that dress off until we get home tonight. You look amazing."

"You do look hot, girl," Paige offered in agreement.

"So, am I going to have to worry about any exes trying to make out with you tonight?" I asked, only half joking.

"Not if you're wearing that dress," Christian said looking over Colin's shoulder.

"Nice, Christian," Paige snapped.

"What?" Christian shrugged his shoulders. "You said something first. Besides, she's screwing my brother, which that makes her like, sister material or something."

"Just shut up," Paige commanded, rolling her eyes.

"Fine—it's settled—the dress stays. Now let's go," Colin ordered.

As we all filed through the doorway I asked, "So who's playing tonight?"

"It's a secret," Colin replied.

"Paige, who's playing?

Paige confirmed Colin's story. "No really, it is a secret. Sometimes a larger band comes to town and they want a smaller show for fun or old time's sake. Whatever the reason, they call up Half Kings for an underground show."

"Do you know who's playing, Colin?" I pressed. It drove me crazy when I was left out of the loop on things.

"I might," he replied.

"Colin always knows who it is, but he wouldn't even tell me this time." Christian was clearly not pleased to be excluded from the inner circle either.

Colin laughed at the response of the group. "You will all see soon enough."

* * *

As soon as we entered the crowded bar, Colin ushered us to the front, seating everyone at a table he must have had reserved. I began to ask more questions about who we might be seeing, but he simply acted like he didn't hear me. I leaned in closer, wanting to make sure he could hear my next statement. "I want to talk to you about something important tonight after the show."

He furrowed his brow, concerned by my words. "Is everything all right?"

"Yeah, I just want to talk about some stuff," I answered. I knew I needed to lock myself into the conversation about my past, about Ashton, or I would chicken out. He nodded, then told me he needed to take care of a few things before the show started, and I watched as he escaped into the crowd.

"I'm going to get drinks—you girls want anything?" Christian asked.

"What are you drinking?" Paige asked in a stern tone, her jaw dropping.

"Jesus, *Mom*, I was going to get a ginger ale if that's all right with you?" he snapped. Based on the exchange, I assumed Paige must have had her suspicions about his recent slip from the proverbial wagon. I hadn't heard anything else from Colin about the matter so I assumed it had only been the single incident. I didn't dare get involved in the conversation based on the looks being exchanged.

"I'm good," I called over the crowd.

"And you can get your own," Christian huffed before Paige could put in her request.

As he walked away, I looked to her, the thoughts going through her mind clearly displayed on her face. "Is everything okay?"

"Huh?" Paige muttered, realizing I was watching her. "Oh, it's fine; he gets in a mood sometimes, that's all."

"I'm sure he'll be fine," I attempted to reassure her.

Paige always wanted to talk about Christian and their relationship, but there was concern in her eyes, and in that moment, it seemed to be the furthest thing she wanted to talk about. "You and Colin seem to be getting pretty hot and heavy."

"Yeah, I still can't believe it," I replied, looking around the bar for any sign of Colin, but he was nowhere to be found. "I swore I wouldn't get serious with a guy while I was away at school, but he—I'm not sure, I guess it's his charm."

"Yeah, charm. Or the fact that he's hot as hell," Paige joked.

"Well, that doesn't hurt," I agreed, grinning foolishly.

"Seriously though, Emmie, I've never seen him like this with someone before." Paige's voice shifted to one of concern. "Are you sure you're in this, too?"

Her question knocked the air out of me. I was a little shocked, that being my friend, she would ask me such a thing. "Why would you ask that?"

"It's like you said, you didn't want anything to do with a boyfriend, and now it's all about Colin. I just don't want to see him get hurt if you change your mind."

Even though she had a valid point, I still felt myself getting defensive. "Look, Colin is the one that convinced me to give us a try. I told him I wasn't ready."

"I get that," Paige said looking over her shoulder, presumably checking up on Christian, who was now headed in our direction with two ginger ales. "I didn't mean anything by it, just forget it."

Setting the extra glass down in front of Paige I saw his lips whisper, 'Sorry babe.' She looked up, smiling, their spat ending with a gentle kiss.

I turned toward the stage, my face still hot from the question Paige had asked me. I couldn't figure out if I was angrier that she thought I would hurt Colin or because I thought I might hurt him.

"And now, ladies and gentlemen, we have a very special treat for you tonight." A man with a very large belly and muttonchops on the sides of his round face took the small stage, yelling into the microphone.

The crowd began to scream, though I wondered why since nobody was supposed to know who this was. "Where's Colin?" I asked, looking back at Paige and Christian. They both shrugged their shoulders.

"For your listening pleasure," the man continued, "I am thrilled to present a band some of you might remember when they were just Wesley Jeremiah."

The crowd erupted into frenzied screams. I searched around once again for Colin, but it was hopeless. Turning back to the stage I attempted to wait for him patiently, becoming increasingly agitated he brought me to a concert, only to abandon me before it even began.

"All right, quiet down. Now for those of you who weren't around back in those days, these boys went on to bigger and better things out in Denver, even though we will always remember their New York days, right folks?"

And again the crowd erupted. I turned toward Paige, only able to mouth, 'who?' She seemed to have the answer, but I couldn't figure out what she was trying to say over the noise.

"The Lumineers!" My stomach flipped, and I suddenly found myself screaming like the rest of the crowd. I loved The Lumineers; they had become a standard part of my playlist while painting. Damn, I wished Colin were there.

A petite woman entered onto the stage, taking her seat behind a cello that was waiting for her. Soon after, the four remaining members joined her, the noise from the crowd causing my ears to pulse. The lead singer grabbed the microphone at the front, center stage, motioning for the crowd to silence. After a moment they obeyed.

"Hello Half Kings!" he shouted, which only caused him to have to wait for the crowd to quiet again. "We are thrilled to be here tonight, and actually, we are here thanks to the effort of one friend. This guy helped us out more than once back in the day. Colin, get out here."

I was certain there must be something wrong with my hearing—that is, until I saw Colin stumble onto stage and into the embrace of the lead singer. I looked back at Paige and Christian in disbelief. They just laughed in response to my expression.

"Colin found out we were in town, and he called me

up with a sob story about how he met a beautiful girl who changed everything for him. After thoroughly heckling the poor bastard he still asked if we could help him woo this lovely bird. Isn't that right, brother?"

Colin leaned into the mic, laughing slightly as the crowd cheered. "The boys, oh and sorry, lovely Neyla as well, agreed to help me express my love for my beautiful Clementine."

There it was—he said my name in front of the room of screaming fans, in front of The Lumineers, and now everyone would be sure to witness my inevitable fainting spell. This couldn't be happening.

"That's her right there in the front. Beautiful, right?" Colin graciously offered me up to the crowd, my face now bright red and extremely warm.

"Stand up, love," one of the bandmates chimed.

"Yes, stand up, baby," Colin agreed.

Wanting the embarrassment to cease, I did as I was asked, the crowd whistling at me in response. All I could think was that everyone in the bar thought how completely overdressed I was.

"Babe, since I met you my life has been so different. Better. I feel alive. I know you're a tough nut to crack, and that's why I want to sing a little song for you," Colin continued.

I decided my only hope to make it through the event would be to focus on Colin, staring only at him, letting the crowd fall away. "You sing?" I mouthed toward him in disbelief.

"Yes, sweetheart, I sing. Perhaps not well, but you're about to find out though. Ready guys?" Colin asked looking back at the group. As soon as they began playing the music I recognized the song: "Stubborn Love," one of my favorites.

When he began I could hear the nerves in his voice, but after only a few words, it faded away. He took a step closer to the edge of the stage, locking eyes with me, and in that moment we were alone. After about half the song passed the rest of the band joined in. This was my life now; I was with a man who would get up in front of a crowd of people and serenade me alongside a band he knew I loved.

"Give it up for Colin Bennett everyone!" the lead singer shouted as the song came to an end. Colin was like a rock star up there, exchanging some sort of handshake only the cool kids could possibly know the sequence of.

Leaping from the stage he scooped me up into his arms, dipping me back, and delivering a passionate kiss. As I broke free, he whispered into my ear, breathing heavily, "I love you."

CHAPTER 18

*C*olin had forgotten about the conversation I wanted to have with him after the concert, and who could blame him? Quite honestly, I had not thought about it again until the next morning. I probably should have rushed to his side in that moment and told him everything, but how could I? He loved me. As much as I didn't want to admit it, I was starting to fall for him. Christmas break was close, and I decided I would tell him then. We would have a lot of time alone, and I knew we could really talk it out.

The idea of telling him I was married before, and that I had driven my husband to suicide, wasn't something that came easily for me. I wanted it to not be my past. It had actually started feeling like it wasn't—like it must have happened to someone else—because there was no way I could feel the way I did with Colin, if that had happened to me.

Monday had come before I was ready for it. My shift in focus was starting to concern me. When I first arrived, all I did was look forward to class, but now, the end of the weekend meant a break in my time with Colin. He was spending more time sleeping at my place than at his own. Tearing myself from his warm arms, forcing my naked body out into the cool morning air, was becoming one of the hardest things I did each day.

I no longer wore Ashton's shirts to bed; I hadn't even seen one in over a month. I kept them hidden away, just as I was trying to do with our story. Colin never wanted to wear clothes to bed. He explained that during the night, he sometimes needed to satisfy urges, which I was more than fine with. I had lost count of the number of times I woke up with his face between my legs, coaxing me into an orgasm.

But on this day, I managed to get up, and despite snow flurries, forced myself to class. The thought of Colin in my bed, waiting for me, propelled me forward throughout the day. As the last class ended, I bounded down the stairs and out the front door. Due to the nasty weather, I even considered a taxi rather than the fifteen-minute walk. Though, with the roads, I was probably looking at a similar travel time for the mile distance.

"Clementine Stirling!" a voice shouted behind me. I froze. I knew the voice, but the name was no longer familiar to me. I left that name behind when I left Ohio in my rearview mirror. How in the hell did William Stryker know that name?

I looked around for a moment, gaining slight comfort from the crowd surrounding us. The last time we saw each other was not under the best of circumstances. I squinted at him through the white haze, the cool flakes pelting me in the face, melting on contact.

"What do you want?" I asked, my voice trembling.

"Don't you want to know how I know that name?" he inquired, trying to taunt me.

"I don't really care how you know that name. I just want you to leave me alone. I thought I made that quite clear," I replied, trying to keep my voice firm. Everything in me wanted to know how he knew my married name, but I was certain I did not want to engage him any more than absolutely necessary.

"I see, then maybe I should go talk to your little boyfriend again. I bet he would like to know all about Clementine Stirling." I could see his glee as he threatened me.

"No!" I exclaimed, immediately regretting the desperation in my voice.

"So he doesn't know," Stryker gathered.

"What do you want?" I asked again.

"We need to talk."

"Just tell me what you want, please."

"There's a coffee shop right down the block. It's freezing out here, so let's go talk there."

"Starbucks?" I scoffed; Colin had definitely turned me into a coffee snob.

"You don't have to drink anything, but we need to talk."

I hesitated.

"It's crowded so you don't have to worry. It's about the Stirlings. You'll want to hear what I have to say," he added.

"How do you know about them?" I asked, watching him nervously.

He didn't answer; instead, he walked past me, crossing the street. I didn't move, but just watched him as he nearly dropped out of sight in the sheet of white. I took a couple steps closer, where I saw him standing in front of the coffee house, waiting for me to join him.

We didn't speak again until he had gotten himself a cup and joined me at the table I was waiting for him at.

"Now, will you tell me what the hell is going on?" I demanded.

"When I met you I told you I do research," he began as he stared at me, eagerly awaiting my reaction to his news.

"Yeah, so…"

"I was doing research—on you."

"What?" I asked as the room began to shift around me. "I don't understand."

"Mr. Stirling hired me."

"Hired you to do what?"

"You see, after you left town, and changed your name, he couldn't shake the feeling that maybe his son's death didn't go exactly like you say it did," Stryker explained, unable, or perhaps unwilling, to wipe the smirk from his face. "So, he sent me here to find out what I could. Get to know you, ask you questions, get to the truth."

"What truth? Ashton blew his brains out goddammit! What else does he want to know?"

"He wants the whole story, which I was trying to figure out until pretty boy got in the way," Stryker snarled.

"Oh my God, you actually think you had a shot? I

ditched you on our date because I thought you were a creep. Jesus, you're thick."

"Watch your mouth, or maybe we'll just go tell him right now about your killer past."

I took a deep breath; the room was now starting to actually spin, and a ringing sprung up in my ears. My mind shifted between the fact that this man before me had lied about who he was, taken me on a supposed date in order to gain information, and the fact my ex-father-in-law was hell bent on getting me to confess something dubious about his son's death. I'd had enough.

"Mr. Stirling wants the truth? Fine. I wasn't coming home from the grocery store like I told everyone. In fact, I had just told Ashton we were over. He told me he was going to do it, but I didn't believe him." I could hardly believe I was actually saying the words. Besides my mother, I had never told anyone what happened that night. The guilt was tiring. I didn't want to feel like I was lying to everyone anymore. "I told him to do what he had to do."

"You told him to kill himself?" Stryker asked, amazed as well by my sudden confession.

"I told him to do what he had to do," I repeated, standing. I looked at Stryker before turning to walk out. "Tell Mr. Stirling whatever you want, but just leave me the hell alone."

"Wait just a minute princess." He jumped to his feet, closing the distance between us. "We're not done. You can tell Prince Charming about who you really are, or I'll do it for you."

"Why? What is it of your business?" I asked. "You got what you came for."

He looked me up and down. I could feel his eyes undressing me, and licking his lips first, he said, "I didn't get everything I came for."

I shivered in disgust. "You can't be serious?"

"Your boyfriend assaulted me. I think I deserve something for all of my pain." He paused, leaning in closer and whispering next to my ear, "Sleep with me, and I won't tell him."

It was as if I had lost all control of my body. Pulling my hand back I released all of my might on his jaw, the slap echoing throughout the coffee shop, an instant audience ensuing. "Are you kidding me? I didn't realize assholes like you actually existed."

"Oh come on, don't act so innocent. I've been watching you for some time now. You clearly aren't thinking about your dead husband with all the time you're spending with your boy toy."

A fire exploded in my stomach, "Screw you." I spat the words at him before I turned and walked out, ignoring the shouting from Stryker behind me, warning me of his wrath. I wanted to get home, climb into my shower, and wash away the mental filth I had just been subjected to. How I could have ever thought that creature was attractive was beyond me.

CHAPTER 19

"*P*lease, will you just tell him I'm sick?" I pleaded through the locked door.

"How long do you think he's going to take that as an answer Emmie? If you won't talk to him, will you please talk to me?" Paige spoke softly from the other side of the door.

"Fine, whatever. I can't talk to him, though," I answered.

"Colin? Yeah, I know. No, she is a hot mess." I pressed my ear to the door, to better hear the one-sided conversation Paige was having on the phone. "No, don't... Because she doesn't want you to see her like this... It's a girl thing, but don't worry, I'll take care of her. When she's done puking her guts out I'll have her call you... Okay, bye."

I pulled open the door giving her a disapproving glare. "Really? Hot mess? Puking my guts out?"

"You're the one who said to tell him you're sick. He would be over here taking care of you if I didn't tell him all that," Paige argued, and she was probably right.

"Thanks, I can't face him right now," I replied, walking to the couch and collapsing onto it in a pile of despair.

Paige stared, studying me intensely. "What is your deal?"

"Nothing," I replied, attempting to dismiss her question.

"Since you started dating Colin, you have been walking around this place looking like a sex pot. You come home today, climb into oversized sweats, and out walks Miss Frumpy," Paige pointed out, the truthfulness striking a little too close to home.

"That's not true. I put these on because it's freezing in this place."

"Hey, your landlord is the boyfriend. Don't look at me," Paige jested. Sitting next to me, she placed her hand on top of mine, the warmth of her touch causing a wave of emotion to flood over me. I wasn't sure if I could contain myself much longer.

"Oh Paige," I moaned.

"You know you'll feel better if you talk about it," she urged, bending over to get me to look her in the face.

"I can't do that," I replied, still managing to avoid eye contact, despite her efforts.

"It can't be that bad. Is it something about Colin?" she probed. I decided to play along to the twenty questions and nodded.

"Okay," she contemplated for a moment. "Did you cheat on him?"

I slapped her in the arm with the back of my free hand. "No! I would never do that."

"Well, I don't know. You're acting like someone died," Paige defended herself.

I gasped, looking up at her in horror.

"Oh my God, that's it. Someone died? Emmie, is it your mom?"

"No, no, she's fine," I replied shaking my hand.

"This is just between us, I promise. You can tell me." I looked at her and saw it in her eyes. I could trust her. She was my friend; I hoped she still would be after I told her the truth.

"You can never tell Colin," I reaffirmed.

"Fine, I won't tell him. What's going on?"

"I've been married before…" I began.

"What?" Paige asked.

"Let me get through all of it, or I won't be able to finish," I instructed, and Paige nodded in response. "I married him right out of high school. I was a nobody, and he was everything in the town I came from. I felt like I was lucky he even wanted me. Anyway, long story short, it was a mistake. He was abusive, and I finally decided I'd had enough."

"Good for you," Paige commended me before covering her mouth, realizing she hadn't let me finish. "Oh, sorry."

"So, the night I told him I was leaving, he was wasted and pulling his same old crap, telling me he was going to change and begging me not to leave him. He must have known I was serious this time because he threatened to kill himself. I didn't believe him, Paige. I never thought he would do it, you have to believe me."

"Oh God, sweetheart," she whispered as I fell into her

arms. I didn't need to say it; she already knew how it ended. "When did all this happen?"

"It's been three and a half years," I answered.

"And Colin doesn't know?" she asked. With my head lying in her lap, she wiped my hair away from my wet cheeks.

"I tried to tell him, but I couldn't. I love him so much. How can I tell him I kept that from him, or worse, I drove my ex to kill himself?"

"Stop right there, Emmie," Paige commanded sharply. "You can't possibly think your ex-husband killing himself was your fault. I think I know you well enough to know you would never do anything that would hurt someone. Colin will understand that, too. You didn't do anything wrong."

"If you say so," I muttered half-heartedly.

"I do say so, and once you tell Colin and he says the same thing as me, you'll see I'm right. Your ex was the one who made the mistake, not you. Colin has to know though, Emmie."

"I know." And I did. "I have to tell him soon, too."

"I agree," Paige said.

I sat up. She had no idea about the urgency of the situation. "No, you don't understand. Do you remember that guy, Stryker?"

"Uh yeah, Stryker the stalker," Paige snarled in disgust.

"Yes! Him. He's not a stalker... well, sort of. He's a private investigator my ex-father-in-law hired. He wanted him to track me down and see if there was more to the story about Ashton. Jesus, Paige, I told him. I told him everything, and if I don't tell Colin, he will."

"Wait, slow down. I don't understand... didn't everyone already know what happened to your ex?" Paige attempted to clarify what had happened that night.

I shook my head, dropping it in shame. "I lied. I wish I would have told everyone then, but I didn't think it mattered. I told everyone I was coming home from the grocery store. Nobody but my mom knows I was ending things with Ashton that night. How could I tell his mom and dad that he told me he was going to do it, but I didn't believe him?"

"You were just trying to spare them... it's not your fault," Paige attempted to comfort me.

"You don't understand. I snapped. I told Stryker. He confronted me after school today and told me who he was. I lost it and told him what happened and that he could tell Ashton's dad but to just leave me alone," I said. Unable to hold the rush of emotions back, they caused my body to shake.

"Hey, that's a good thing. Now they'll know the truth, and you don't have to be the one to do it."

"He said he's going to tell Colin unless—" The words stuck in my throat.

"Unless what?" Paige inquired hesitantly.

I wiped the tears away, trying to regain my composure. "Unless I sleep with him."

"What? What a slime-ball!" Paige yelled. "Then you need to tell Colin, and that's all there is to it."

"Can it wait until tomorrow? I don't know if I can handle it right now." I don't know why I felt the need to ask for permission to wait. Maybe I wanted her to confirm it wasn't because I was afraid, but rather I

182

deserved the night's rest before jeopardizing my relationship with the first man I had managed to love again.

"First thing in the morning, all right?" Paige
confirmed. For one more night, Colin would think I was
the woman of his dreams before I ruined everything with
the truth.

CHAPTER 20

The moment my phone began to vibrate I knew it would be Colin's smoldering image on the screen. I had been preparing myself all morning for the call, and during my braver moments I even considered calling him myself, but of course that never happened. I waited for a few more bars of the "Stubborn Love" ringtone to chime before swiping the phone with my finger and lifting it to my ear.

"Hello," I whispered, playing up the sick story from the night before.

"Babe? Are you all right?" he asked immediately.

I cleared my throat. There didn't need to be any more lies between us. "Yeah, I'm better today."

"Thank God. I was so worried when I didn't hear from you." I could hear the genuine concern in his voice. I imagined him the night before, pacing in his loft, thinking about me, wanting to do anything to help make me better. The guilt actually made me shiver. I hated it; I couldn't see him because I was having trouble telling him the truth—

the truth about who I really was. The lies kept building, and I had put him through enough.

In that instant I knew if I didn't get this over with soon, I would probably never tell him. "Are you busy?"

"I was planning on coming over there and taking care of you all day," Colin informed me, trying to make sure I understood his caretaking wasn't an option.

"I told you, I'm fine," I reiterated, wishing he would quit saying things that only made the guilt linger.

"I'll be the judge of that," Colin said, unrelenting.

I paused. How could I say this to him? It was excruciating enough telling Paige about it. But she didn't hate me... I had told her everything, and she still loved me as much as ever. Paige hadn't given herself to me in the way Colin had, though. She hadn't shared the most intimate details of the painful times in her life with me. How could he possibly not hate me for hiding these things from him? It needed to be in person—that much was for certain. "Can you come over?"

"Be right there." And then he was gone—the line clicked, and it was dead. My heart started racing. This was it. He was coming straight over. There would be no more avoiding my past.

Looking down at the oversized pajama pants hanging from my hips, stained tank top, and sweatshirt draped over my frame I decided it was time for some fast-acting primping. If I was about to obliterate the perfect image Colin had of me in his mind, I at least needed to look like something he wanted to hold onto.

Rushing to the dresser, I left my dirty clothes in a pile on the floor, stripping them off like they were a layer of dead skin. I grabbed a pair of black leggings from the second drawer, and slid them on as quickly as possible. Next to where the leggings had been was one of my favorite thrifty finds—a knee-length, bulky knit, taupe sweater with a scoop neck that fell to one side, exposing a bare shoulder.

There was no time for a major hair makeover, so in a quick dash to the bathroom I grabbed a brush, and gritting my teeth, I forced it through the tangles. It wasn't perfection, but it would have to do. The mascara residue under my eyes, however, would have to go. Licking my fingertips I wiped any sign of the previous night's cry fest away.

Walking into the living room I began considering where might be the best place to have the conversation. Paige had left for an early morning fashion shoot. I had heard her complaining from the comfort of my bed. Apparently the photographer had been waiting for a good snow to do the shoot. Half naked in a snowy public park seemed like a less than ideal job to me. No matter how much that girl complained, though, I knew she loved it.

Shouting outside the window suddenly interrupted my thoughts. I had become accustomed to the noises of New York, but this was a little too close for comfort, and I instantly began worrying Colin might end up collateral damage in whatever the confrontation was. Leaning over, I peered out the window, and much to my horror I realized the source of the shouting was, in fact, Colin. He was in an altercation with someone who was out of my eyesight.

I wasted no time fleeing out the apartment door, scurrying down the steps, and bursting from the security door. When I saw Stryker in Colin's grip, it was like the air got knocked out of me.

"Em!" Colin shouted, looking to my bare feet. "Get back inside."

"What's going on?" I cried, my mind having trouble processing the scene.

Colin shoved Stryker to the ground, taking a step back. "Nothing, except this guy can't seem to take a hint."

It was too late; the truth was catching up to me before I could find a way to share it. I shook my head no, and more than anything I wanted to rewind, to go back to the night before and do as Paige told me and go straight over to Colin to tell him everything.

"Em, I'm serious. You have to get inside. You don't even have any shoes on," Colin said sternly, narrowing his brow in my direction.

"No, you come with me," I pleaded, stepping up and down repeatedly to make the cold more tolerable on my bare feet.

"Wait, no!" Stryker said climbing to his feet. "He's not going anywhere until he hears what I have to say."

Colin turned from me, glaring at the man that stood across from him in utter disgust. "You have nothing I want to hear. Now go."

My stomach twisted in knots, and my head began to spin. *Please, please God, just let him walk away. Leave us alone. Let me tell him myself. I promise, I will never keep anything from him again. Walk away.* I wanted to shout, but I stood silent, helpless.

"What I've got to say, you'll be glad you listened."

Stryker's words were like venom. He was obviously bitter about the repeated beatings and rejections.

"Please William, just go," I squeaked out. My voice caused Colin to freeze; he heard something in it that gave him pause. He stared at me, his beautiful eyes widening, his brow was no longer furrowed. Instead, he looked at me with utter confusion, and for an instant I thought I might actually see fear in his gaze. He could see I had a secret.

"Did you tell him anything, Clementine?" Stryker asked in my direction.

"Tell me what?" Colin demanded, not taking his eyes from me.

I couldn't look at him. I stared at the ground, wishing somehow Stryker would simply evaporate before he could say another word, but he didn't. He kept going, and I just stood there—silent—unable to think of a single thing to say.

"So, she didn't tell you about our little meeting yesterday?" Stryker was positively reveling in delight as he shredded my biggest hope I'd had in as long as I could remember.

"Em, say something. What is he talking about?" Colin cried, the hurt on his face was too much for me to take. I shook my head. I couldn't have this conversation—not like this. It was too hard as it was, and now with Stryker badgering me, it was simply more than I could handle.

"I can't believe this. You two can have each other," Colin said, waving his hands in my direction and turning to walk away.

He didn't understand. It was obvious he thought I was

cheating on him with Stryker. How could he think I
would even do that to him?

"Colin!" I finally shouted. I could feel everything I had
come to love slipping away from me. It was too late; he
wasn't turning back—he was gone. I'd lost him. Ruined
this. Just like I thought, I broke people.

I had forgotten about my feet, which made sense
considering I could no longer feel them. Stryker went on,
saying a few things to me, but I really wasn't listening by
that point—everything had faded into a numb buzzing
sound. I turned and walked back into my building, leaving
William shouting nonsense behind me like a mad man.
None of it mattered now that Colin hated me.

CHAPTER 21

*T*he past week had been a blur. When I first got back into the apartment after the altercation between Stryker and Colin, I managed to work up the courage to call him. Correction: I called him seven times, but he never answered, and a message didn't seem appropriate. With the last call I decided to leave one—a simple, 'I'm sorry.'

By the time Paige had gotten back from her job I was already packed. Of course she grilled me, demanding every detail. She seemed to think everything could be explained away, and I only needed to give Colin time to cool down. After he realized I hadn't cheated on him, my past would seem like nothing in comparison.

Perhaps she was right, but I needed time to think it through. Part of me kept telling myself I should have never been with Colin. I knew when I came to New York that I was broken, and that was why I had sworn off love. It was inevitable, I would end up getting hurt and everyone around me seems to end up as collateral damage.

I decided to head home for Christmas break three days early, confident my mother would be able to piece some part of me back together. I couldn't take seeing Colin at the coffee shop or around the apartment while I was trying to work through my feelings for him. I was certain when I returned after the first of the year enough time would have passed that I could handle the casual encounters.

I had sworn Paige to secrecy again before I left. Trying to convince myself a clean break would be best for everyone, I knew the easiest way for this to work would be for Colin to hate me. As long as he thought I cheated on him, I wouldn't have to worry about the charming Colin coming around, trying to fix things between us.

When I got home my mother smiled and hugged me, genuinely happy to see me, but she could see the pain I was in. She listened as I told her everything; she had always been that person for me, even when everything with Ashton happened. I don't know if it was because my dad left us when I was young, but we had always been close like that. The comfort I had longed for on the flight home wasn't there when I arrived. Telling her all of my woes relieved none of my pain.

"It's him again," my mom said, looking at my phone.

"Don't answer it," I replied, staring blankly.

"You've been home for a week now. The two of you have both had time to cool off—maybe talking will do you good."

"No, I said I don't want to talk to him," I added firmly.

"You're my daughter, and I'll do as you ask, but even I can see he feels something very special for you," my mom said, standing and running her fingers through my hair.

I didn't respond. I knew Colin loved me, so that wasn't my problem. The issue was that I loved Colin, too, and I couldn't stomach the thought of doing to him what I had done to Ashton. I committed myself to Ashton, gave him my vows, told him I would be there forever. If walking out on him wasn't enough, I basically told him to pull the trigger. I used people until there was nothing left of them. I wouldn't do that to Colin.

Mom was my mother, so of course she would always be the one to tell me it wasn't my fault, but she was blinded by bias. She couldn't see the disease I was to the people around me. I just barely came into Colin's life, and it had already started. I didn't want to hurt him, but I always managed to find a way to hurt the people I cared about. It was simply who I was. I needed to get out of the relationship with him while he still had a piece of who he was.

Another minute passed, and the phone began to vibrate again. "He's not going away," my mom called from the other room.

Frustrated, I sat up, and without much thought I swiped my finger across the bar and pulled the phone up to my ear. For a moment we both sat in silence. At last Colin spoke, "Em?"

I didn't reply. The sound of his voice made my stomach flutter, and I thought I might actually vomit. Instead I listened, waiting for him to unleash his fury on me. I needed to hear it; I wanted him to scream at me, to tell me what a whore I was, even though I hadn't let another man touch me. I wanted something to make it easier to hate him back.

"Well, I'll assume by the breathing I hear that you're on the other end of the line, Em. We need to talk. I shouldn't have stormed off like I did. I didn't give you a chance to explain, and that was wrong. I'm sorry." Why wasn't he shouting at me? Damn it, Colin.

"We're over," I replied flatly.

"Please don't say that." His voice sounded strained, and I wondered if he had gotten much sleep in the past week. I know I hadn't. "I love you, Em. I want to try and figure this out… no matter what happened. Don't just give up on us."

There it was, the Colin that I had trouble saying no to. I was glad I had decided to fly home, because I knew if that conversation had happened face to face, I would not have been able to resist him. I took a deep breath in. I needed this to stop because I couldn't resist much more. "Don't call here again."

Instead of ending the call, I powered down my phone. There couldn't be any further communication between us right now. I wasn't ready for it.

My mom stood several feet behind me, staring at me until at last she said, "I hope you know what you're doing."

Christmas was two days away, and then New Year's would come and go, so by the time I returned to New York Colin's desperation would twist into anger. Anger I could handle.

* * *

CHAPTER 22

I shifted the packages around, pulling one out of the bag after the next; I came across one I had gotten for Paige. In the frenzy to get home, I grabbed the bag of gifts, not taking the time to sort out the ones for my mom. I continued pulling items out of the bag until the entire tree was surrounded.

I then began repacking the items I needed with me to return back to New York: a cowl-neck scarf for the ever-fashionable Christian and some exquisite vintage jewelry for Paige, which I was certain she was going to love. Staring at the final box my heart sank. I missed him; I didn't want to, but I did. The last box was for Colin. Pushing it into the bag with the other items I attempted to shove him from my mind.

"Oh, Emmie!" my mom squealed as she walked into the living room, the gifts under the tree coming into view. "Please tell me you didn't break the handmade gifts only rule."

"All right, now I promise like ninety percent of the

stuff is handmade, but I saw something at this flea market, and it was so you that I had to get it. I suppose it qualifies, though, since the girl I bought it from made it."

"You shouldn't spoil me so much," my mom protested.

"You're my mom, it's kind of my job," I replied with a grin.

"Your gifts are in the sunroom," she noted. "Just let me go and—" she was interrupted by a knock at the door.

"Want me to get it?" I asked standing to my feet.

"It's probably Billy. I'll get it. Your gifts are on the table under the window. Would you mind grabbing them and slipping them under the tree?" she asked.

Billy was the newest resident at The Grove and since coming home, I discovered he had been spending a lot of time with my mother. He seemed very nice, but with his longer hair and full beard it sometimes felt like I was looking at the cover of one of my mom's albums from the seventies. I was glad she had met someone though; I hated the idea of her being lonely while I was away.

Retrieving the gifts, I walked into the living room and slid them under our Charlie Brown-like tree. "Mom, you ready to open some gifts, lady?"

"Emmie," I heard her soft voice from the opposite side of the room. Turning to look at her I could see something was concerning her.

"Is everything all right?" I asked, standing. When I stood I saw a sight over her shoulder, and I thought my eyes were deceiving me. Paige and Christian were standing in the entryway, smiles beaming back at me.

I hesitated for a moment. "Hey girl, Merry Christmas!" Paige yelled.

"Oh my God! What are you doing here?" I cried, rushing over and collapsing into her open arms.

After a moment of screaming and jumping in place we finally managed to pull away from each other long enough for her to answer me. "You didn't think I was going to have Christmas without my bestie, did you?"

"Are they always like this?" my mother asked, looking over at Christian.

"You have no idea. I think she likes your daughter more than her own boyfriend." Christian laughed.

"Can you blame her?" I asked with a half-smile. "I'm positively adorable.

My heart was still racing; I couldn't believe she was actually here. No matter what I was going through with Colin, nothing changed what had developed between Paige and me.

"Emmie..." Paige began. I looked to her, sensing the hesitation.

"Is everything okay?" I asked. Based on her sudden change in facial expression, I immediately began thinking of the worst possible scenarios. My thoughts shifted to Colin—he was the only reason she would look at me that way. I was certain the curse of Clementine had landed him in the hospital, or worse. I hadn't ended things soon enough obviously.

"Don't kill me," she said raising her hands defensively. With that, I knew he was safe, but Paige might not be very shortly.

"What did you do?" I demanded.

"I may have told Colin a few things that you told me

not to," Paige whispered, wincing when she finished her sentence, waiting for me to unleash holy hell on her.

But I didn't because part of me was glad he knew, though I would never tell Paige that. "What did you say to him?"

She looked over at Christian and then to my mother uncomfortably. "Not much... He was flipping out after you hung up on him a couple nights ago, and he kept trying to call you back. He had it in his head you were with that Stryker creep and that was why you weren't answering your phone."

"Are you serious? That's disgusting," I snapped. It was becoming apparent that perhaps Colin didn't know anything about me.

"Right? So you see why I had to set him straight."

"Oh Lord, Paige," I groaned. "Tell me everything you told him."

"Not much, I swear. I told him he had it all wrong, and the minute he knew I had information he was relentless," Paige stammered.

"Yeah. He can be that way," I agreed.

"Tell me about it," Christian interjected, obviously feeling slightly uncomfortable discussing his brother in the den of women.

"I told him he had it all wrong about Stryker and that he was a private investigator hired by your husband's parents," she explained.

"You didn't!" I cried, the horror of it all on my face.

"Okay, I admit, that didn't go over very well," Paige continued. "I told him you're not married anymore, but that I couldn't tell him anything else."

Christian leaned forward. "That's when he decided we would all have to fly to Indiana during one of the most highly travelled holidays. That was awesome, by the way."

"Shut up, Christian," Paige said, delivering an elbow to his unsuspecting ribs.

"Wait, what? All? Colin came out with you?" My high from seeing my best friend on Christmas morning quickly faded into pure panic as I found out my ex was not far away.

Paige nodded, widening her eyes innocently. "He's waiting for you by the car."

Without a word I rushed to the front of the house, pulling the oversized cardigan I was wearing closer around my body and glancing out the front window. Sure enough, he was leaning against a black rental sedan, his ankles crossed, his face tucked down into his pea coat to avoid the harsh wind.

"No, he can't—you have to get him out of here. I can't talk to him," I pleaded, turning back to the three sets of eyes staring at me.

Christian stepped forward. "Emmie, I have never seen my brother like this before. I don't think I could drag him out of here."

"I know it's scary sweetheart," my mother added, her face masked with concern.

"It's terrifying. If I go out there I might not be able to say no. I'm not ready for this. I need more time," I moaned. All I could think about was crawling back into my bed, pulling the blankets over my head, pushing it all away. My face was suddenly hot, and I could feel the moisture building up behind my lids, close to tears already.

Lovingly, my mother picked up a jacket that was lying across the back of a chair near the door. She draped it over my shoulders and squeezed my arm gently. Coming close to my ear she whispered, "You can do this."

I smiled. She had been my strength for so long. She picked me up when I had decided it hurt too much to continue breathing. She was the one who reminded me survival was just putting one foot in front of the other. She had survived so much pain herself, I couldn't keep bringing my mess and dropping it in her lap.

Taking a deep breath, I made up my mind and opened the front door. Nobody said a word as I exited. I'm not sure if it was because they didn't want to spook me, or if they simply didn't know what to say.

As I approached him, I could see him stiffen, stand upright, and pull his strong jaw from the shelter of his coat. He smiled with only half of his mouth, and I felt my knees go weak. We both stayed quiet, neither sure who should speak the first word. I came to rest next to him, turning to look back at the modest, wooden framed home, pressing my back against the car to give me support.

"Merry Christmas." Colin was the first to mutter words. I smiled; it was so Colin to open like that.

"What are you doing here?" I asked, deciding to stick with playing it cool.

"Paige said some things that needed some clarity, and well, honestly, I needed to see your face. Your mom was nice enough to email me her address," Colin explained.

"What?" The loving woman who always had my back had already taken sides. I had been double-crossed.

"Em, I love you. I don't care about anything else other than being with you. Don't you get that?" I couldn't look at him as he spoke—it was killing me.

"You have no idea who I am. How can you say you love me?" I pushed back.

He turned toward me, trying to get me to look at him, but I still refused. "So tell me then, I'm listening. What is so terrible about you that I wouldn't love you? That you've been married before? Paige told me. I'm not scared off that easily."

He needed me to give him the cold, hard truth if he was going to let go of me. I faced him, looking up into his pained eyes. Damn it. That was a mistake. How can he look so damn sexy and sad at the same time. "You want to know who I am? All the wretched details? Would that make you happy?"

"All I've ever wanted is to get to know you. I don't think anything you ever did would be as terrible as you think. At least not in my eyes."

"We'll see," I began, starting to tremble as I spoke. "I was married. I got married right after high school, actually."

"Emmie, a lot of people make that mistake." Colin's attempts to console me were only making me angry. The fact that he thought a simple divorce would be what upset me this much made me realize how much this information was going to level him.

"Damn it, Colin, do you want to know or not?" I snapped, shifting my eyes wildly as I struggled not to cry.

He nodded.

"His name was Ashton. A couple years in, the cracks started showing. I tried, but things just got worse. We were both miserable, even if he wasn't willing to admit it. One night, he was wasted—he could barely stand. I told him I was done. He begged me, he cried. I didn't care. I didn't care about anything except myself, and what I wanted. I was finally being selfish. I'd given him too much of myself for far too long. I wanted freedom—from him, from that God-forsaken suffocating small town. He told me if I left him he would kill himself. He had said it so many times I didn't believe him. It was how he controlled me."

As I retold the night I could see the scene unfolding as if it had only happened moments ago. I flinched as I heard the gun shot ring out in my thoughts. I couldn't say the words to him. I couldn't tell Colin that I drove a man I once loved to kill himself. How could I possibly tell the man I now loved that I was a murderer?

"Scre, Em," Colin whispered, pulling me close to him, resting his chin on the top of my head. He was so warm, I told myself to push him away, but my body wasn't listening. "I'm so sorry you had to go through that, baby."

"Don't you get it? I'm the reason he's dead," I moaned, digging my face deeper into his chest, unable to stop the flood of sobs.

"No, you're the reason I'm alive," Colin whispered, pulling away slightly and lifting my face, our eyes locking. Pressing his thumbs against my ice cold dampened cheeks he wiped away my tears, pressing his lips to mine. I sniffed, barely able to breath from the crying fit, but losing the oxygen was worth it. His lips parted mine, instantly warming my body all over, despite the chill around us.

When our lips separated it felt like a piece of my own soul was being torn away. I wanted to surround myself with him, wear him like a coat that would protect me from all of the pain in the world. "You don't hate me?" I asked in disbelief.

Colin laughed softly. "I'm crazy about you, Em. I could *never* hate you."

I shook my head. "You don't understand... I'm cursed. If you're with me it will mean you only end up getting hurt."

Colin took a firm hold of my arms, staring at me intensely. "Listen to me. My life started when you gave us a chance. Don't take that away from either of us."

It was no use—there were parts of me shouting to stay strong, but he was here, looking into my eyes, touching me. His presence created a helpless hunger in me I couldn't resist. He was doing exactly what I knew he would if I saw him face to face. I was literally swooning.

"Well, I did already get you a Christmas gift." I wondered if I had actually just said those ridiculous words.

He released a husky laugh, pleased with the progress he was making with me. "Oh yeah? What did you get me?"

Yup, I had said it.

"I brought it with me, actually," I added, slipping my arm into his as we started walking toward the house.

"What is it?" he asked, clearly puzzled. But before I

could answer he quickly asked, "Wait, so you knew I'd come after you? Is that what you're saying?"

"I know everything, don't you know that?" I retorted playfully. It was clear to me that Colin wasn't going to let me get rid of him easily, and perhaps, if I were honest with myself for a moment, I didn't want to let him go. I just needed to figure out how to get the rest of me to stop thinking about Ashton anytime I thought I might be experiencing a little too much happiness.

"I forget sometimes," he said with a smile. Before we even reached the front porch the door flew open and an audience who had clearly been watching the entire show from the window greeted us.

"Our address, Mom? Really?" I asked, giving the woman who had given me life an evil stare.

"What? I don't know what you're talking about. Now get in here before you freeze."

CHAPTER 23

"*A*re you ever going to take that thing off from around your neck?" I asked, grabbing a hold of the chain and giving it a yank.

Colin pulled away from me defensively, shielding his precious treasure. "Um—never!" he exclaimed.

I laughed, thrilled by my excellent Christmas gift giving skills. The idea struck me about a week after the show with The Lumineers. Colin and his brother were playing around on their guitars, yet another talent I didn't know he possessed, when my love started complaining about his cheap pick.

I remembered seeing an artisan at the local crafters' market who created custom metal stamped items. After a little searching on the internet I ordered a silver pick with the words 'Stubborn Love' engraved on it. The woman even offered to add a punch hole so it could be worn on a chain. While I thought that was an excellent idea, I was surprised he hadn't taken it off for five days straight.

"You're crazy," I replied lightly, laying my head against his chest.

"Are you excited about your gift at all?" Colin asked, as I watched his chest moving up and down. Snuggling together on his oversized couch had become one of my favorite things to do.

"Seriously? How can you even ask that? Although you spent too much," I reminded him.

"How do you know how much I spent? Maybe I got a great deal," Colin teased.

"Because I know even with a deal a giant European-style easel was too expensive."

"You love it, though?" he asked again.

I thought about his question for a moment. "You know what I like best about it?"

"What's that?" he asked.

"It smells like you," I replied, breathing him in deeply.

Amused, his chest vibrated as he laughed. "And what exactly do I smell like?"

"Wood," I quickly answered.

Leaning forward and cocking his head, he attempted to get a better look at my face, but I wasn't about to budge from my comfortable spot, using him as my pillow. "Wood, really? I smell like wood." He sniffed his shoulders for a trace of the odor.

"It's not a bad thing. I love it. I think it's a construction smell."

"A construction smell, huh?" he teased, a sarcastic expression on his face.

"Are you making fun of me?" I asked, pretending to be angry.

"Never."

"Speaking of construction, I still can't believe how much you got done on this place the week I was gone." I glanced around the open room; the walls had been finished and painted a pristine white. The kitchen was completed, including the subway tile backsplash. The only thing they were waiting on was the marble slab on the island to be installed.

"I told you, as soon as you left I couldn't sleep. What else was I supposed to do?"

"It really is beautiful, babe," I stated, running my fingertips up and down his arm, which hung over my shoulder.

"It will be even more beautiful when you get your paintings in here... or am I going to have to find a new painter for hire?" Colin attempted to goad me.

"I'm just waiting to see if I'm chosen for the gallery project," I replied matter of fact.

Lowering his brow, he questioned, "Why does that matter?"

"Because if my work is picked, it means my prices for you will go up dramatically."

Dropping his jaw in shock, I was suddenly over-whelmed by his firm tickling fingers, wrapping and working their way across my midsection. "Oh, is that right?"

I squealed, then panted and begged for a reprieve, but he wouldn't relent.

"Oh God, they're at it again," Christian moaned as he and Paige walked into the main living area.

Breaking free from Colin's grasp, I fled to the other

end of the couch, attempting to catch my breath.

"Hey you two, what are you guys up to tonight?" Colin asked, sounding very fatherly, but not removing his eyes from me.

"Well, we had hoped to stay in and watch a movie, but it looks like you guys have the couch pretty much monopolized," Christian growled.

"Wow, someone's in a mood," Colin commented, glancing back at his brother.

"He's been like this all day," Paige added, walking past him.

"Like what?" Christian demanded.

"Why don't we all hang out and watch a movie together?" I suggested, attempting to change the subject.

"Great, I'll make popcorn," Paige said walking into the kitchen. "Oh, Emmie, that box set of Cards Against Humanity just came in... you want to run over to our place and grab them?"

"Sure," I replied, standing.

"Yes!" Christian said raising his hands above his head as if to indicate a score. "Some C-A-H would totally rock."

"Am I the only person in the world who hasn't played this yet?" Colin asked looking around the room.

After a brief moment of silence Christian was pleased to be the one to confirm, "Yeah bro, you might be the lamest dude I know."

"Ha ha, real funny. You want me to go with you, hon?" Colin asked as I slid my feet into my oversized rain boots.

"Nah, I'll be right back. Keep my spot warm," I instructed, turning and rushing out the door. Colin and I had been inseparable since the flight home. When I was with him I didn't think about Ashton or his family. I certainly didn't think about Stryker. I only had another week before school was starting back up, and I wanted to spend as much time as possible with him.

Slipping my key into the security door, I took the stairs two by two, eager to return to my beloved's side. When I reached the hall my breath caught in my throat, and I instantly froze. Standing just outside my door, staring at me with the same eyes as his son was Ashton's father.

"Clementine," he said softly, shifting his weight from foot to foot. For an older gentleman, Robert was quite handsome. Ashton had his mom's hair color, but the rest of him was all his father.

"Mr. Stirling, what are you doing here?" I asked, my voice trembling.

"When I told your downstairs neighbor I was your father-in-law she was nice enough to let me in. Curious thing, though, she asked when you and Colin got married."

I didn't know why I suddenly felt like a teenager, explaining myself, as if I had done something wrong. "I'm sorry Mr. Stirling. I know I should have stayed in better contact."

"I understand, child. I'd like to talk to you, if you don't mind. Could I come in?" he asked.

I hesitated; the idea of being alone with him after what Stryker must have told him scared me. "My friends are waiting for me."

"I won't be long, and I've come a long way. Could you give a few minutes to someone who used to be family?"

Suddenly I remembered there was so much more Ashton and his father had in common—they were both excellent at manipulating people.

"Of course," I relented, unlocking the door, allowing him to enter first. I followed him to the living room, waiting for him to sit, but he did not. Instead he stood near the window, staring out into the night street.

"Nice place you have here, Clementine," he added, glancing in my direction. I stood behind the couch, wanting with every fiber of my being to duck down and hide behind it.

"Thank you, I live here with my room mate, P—"

"Yes, Paige. Well, you know I already know all of these things," Mr. Stirling continued. "It seems silly to pretend otherwise."

"Yes, about that. I'm not really sure why you would think you had to go to such drastic measures. If you had any questions I would have been happy to answer them for you." What I actually wanted to do was scream at the man, tell him that he had set a psychopath loose on me. But I couldn't. I knew he was just hurting, confused by what Ashton had done, and like the rest of us, he was trying to find a way to move on.

"I'm not so sure about that, Clementine. You and your mom leave town with barely a word. I find out you reverted back to your maiden name. Your mom doesn't answer our correspondence. What's a man to think?" His questions were pointed, his stare cold.

"I know I could have handled things better—so many times I thought about picking up the phone and calling Maggie... I mean, Mrs. Stirling. I wasn't sure what to say,"

I explained, wishing he knew how sincerely I had not wished to perpetuate their pain. We were all grieving in our own way.

"It broke her heart, Clementine. She lost her only son, and then when you disappeared it was like losing a daughter, too."

"I know, and I said I'm sorry."

"Seems like you're sorry about a lot of things. At least that's what you say." Robert took a step closer and my heart began to race.

"I'm not sure what you mean." I shifted uncomfortably in my galoshes.

"Stryker told me what you said happened that night with Ashton. That you told him he should go ahead and kill himself. Are you sorry about that, Clementine?"

I had never hated my name more than when I heard him speak it, the loathing sent chills down my spine. "You have no idea how much I regret the way that happened. I've thought about it every day. I didn't think he was serious," I stammered through the excuses.

"Yeah, it seems you're really broken up. So you think about him when you're shacked up with this Colin character?"

"It's not like that," I insisted. With each step he moved toward me, I matched with my own step backward until at last my back was pressed against the wall.

"Please, sir. You have to believe me. I loved Ashton. If I had known—"

"Don't you dare desecrate his memory by saying you loved him," he growled, now only inches away from me. I couldn't speak; the same fear I had once felt at the hands of his son I was experiencing in that moment. Grabbing hold of my arms he shook me, a fire in his eyes as he shouted, "You'll see. I'm going to have you brought up on murder charges. We'll see how happy you and your little boy wonder are then."

"Please, I didn't—" I begged, tears running down my cheeks. I closed my eyes, wishing it were over.

"You were never good enough for him. Some stupid town slut—I told him—but would he listen, no."

I opened my eyes and watched in horror as he drew his hand back, preparing to strike me, the rage in his eyes causing me to squeeze them shut once again. I preferred the darkness rather than the way I was reflected in those despair filled pools.

The strike against my cheek caused a ringing in my ears, which for a moment deafened all other sounds. In a way it was a relief, as I couldn't hear his venomous shouts any longer. I fell to the floor, curling into a tight ball, attempting to close so tightly into myself, he might decide I wasn't worth the effort.

As the ringing stopped I heard flesh colliding with flesh and the scuffling of shoes across the wooden floor. It was Colin; he was deflecting a punch from Mr. Stirling. I didn't move, but rather watched in silent horror as the man I currently loved twisted the arm of the father of the man I once loved, shoving him into the kitchen area and out the front door.

Seconds later Colin was scooping me into his arms, frantically pulling the hair from my face. "Em? Are you okay? Answer me, Em. Come on, baby. I need you to give me a sign you're all right."

I nodded, pressing my head into him, releasing all of the pain into his chest. I reached up and grabbed his shoulder, tightening my grasp on him. I wanted to dig my fingers into him, make myself part of him. If I could join with him, maybe I could be strong enough for this.

CHAPTER 24

The sun peeked through the curtains as the smell of coffee filled the apartment. Slowly, I reached up, rubbing the sleep that had crystalized at the corner of my eyes during the night. My eyes were tender and my throat raw from all of the tears.

Colin spent most of the night trying to reassure me. He told me how it was impossible for me to be held responsible for Ashton's death, and that Mr. Stirling was merely trying to lash out in any way he could. I was an easy target. It didn't matter if Colin was right or wrong. I was tired of feeling guilty; maybe it was time I was held accountable.

"Morning, beautiful," Colin said, walking into my room carrying a tray. Sitting up I feigned a smile.

"I'm sure I look ravishing."

"You do to me." He placed the tray across the end of the bed. Coffee, toast, eggs, slightly burnt turkey bacon, and a mix of fruit overflowed from a plate. "Apparently you girls don't believe in real bacon?"

"I do, but Paige won't allow it. She already isn't happy I bring actual bread into the house," I explained, rolling my eyes to express my disapproval of the restrictions.

"This from the same girl I have seen put away a cheeseburger and an entire plate of french fries?" Colin laughed.

I shrugged. "I didn't say she made sense."

"Well, I hope you enjoy this. I did the best I could," he said, leaning over and kissing my forehead. I watched as he walked around, taking a seat next to me.

"Thanks, it looks great," I said, pulling the tray closer and picking at the contents.

"Are you feeling better today?" I could feel his eyes staring at me as I attempted to eat a few scraps.

"Not really."

"I'm sorry last night was so hard on you, baby. That wasn't fair of him to put all of that on you." I felt Colin's broad hand settle on my back, sweeping from side to side.

"I don't see how you can say it's not fair."

"What do you mean?" he asked, confused.

"You wouldn't understand," I dismissed, only able to muster a whisper as I spoke.

"I'm here because I want to understand, so help me, please. How is anything that happened last night fair to you? It was total bullshit in my opinion." Colin stopped rubbing my back and stared at me, waiting for me to give him a hint of what was going through my mind.

"He's right," I answered, hoping he would take that as enough of an answer and leave me in peace to continue wallowing in my self-pity. Which was something I had become quite an expert at over the years.

"Who?" Colin questioned, and when he saw I had no intention of answering him he continued, "You can't be serious? Let me see if I've got this straight—you're telling me that you think your dead husband's father coming here, years later, and threatening you is somehow justified? Em, he's an asshole, and he had no right to put you through all of that again."

I wanted him to leave. More than anything, I knew he was trying to make things better, but I didn't want them to be better. I wanted to hate myself; I wished he could see how much I deserved everyone's loathing. Sitting up, I looked into his eyes. "His son is dead because of me. I think he has every right."

"His son is dead because he shot himself. You need to stop blaming yourself," Colin argued I could see he wanted to reach out and touch me, but was hesitant.

"I told him to do it!" I cried, struggling to not come completely unraveled.

When he could no longer keep his distance, Colin reached out and took my hand into his, squeezing it tight. I stared into his eyes. "I don't care what you said to him, this was not your fault. For someone to take their own life, they were in a place that can't be the fault of any one person. You told me about how he mistreated you. I think if a man believes there is something acceptable about that behavior, there is inherently something wrong with him. Based on the way his father treated you, I am guessing the apple didn't fall too far from the tree."

"His son is dead, you shouldn't say—"

Colin didn't wait for me to finish, "I shouldn't speak the truth? He hit you! He's lucky I didn't kill him."

"I guess we'll see. He said he was going to report this to the police. If I'm guilty, I'm sure it won't take them long to come knocking," I noted.

Colin laughed at the notion. "There is absolutely no way anyone is going to even listen to him. When you made that statement to Ashton, you didn't believe he had any intention of actually hurting himself. He had a history of abuse with you, there was no weapon in his hand when you left, and he was not in a state of mind that made you feel safe. Mr. Stirling is hurting, so he's trying to blame someone because it's easier than thinking his son was in some way defective. Any cop will see that."

I didn't speak at first—I knew Colin was right. I knew legally I hadn't done anything wrong. I couldn't shake the feeling, though, that it wasn't fair for me to be happy. Ashton would never be able to be happy again. Anything other than a life of misery felt like I was being selfish. I wanted to be with Colin, but I didn't know how to set things right. If I can't give him all of me, it isn't fair to let him throw his heart away.

And then I made a decision. "I'm going to Ohio."

"What?" Colin nearly choked on the word.

"I need to go and talk to his mother. She deserves to know everything that happened that night... from me," I explained, staring at a blank space on the wall in order to avoid his eyes, even though I could feel them burning through my cheek.

"That's not a good idea," he quickly added.

"I need to do it," I stated flatly.

"Em! That won't change anything. You're not going," he insisted.

This was not something Colin was going to be able to talk me out of. I had made up my mind. Turning my head to meet his eyes so there would be no mistaking me, I replied, "I'm going to Ohio. You don't need to understand; in fact, it doesn't even fully make sense to me, but I know I need to go, as much for us as for them.

I could see the fear in his eyes. The loss of control of something he found precious, slipping out of his fingertips. Then he surprised me, "Fine, I'm going with you."

"No, you're not, I need to do this on my own," I argued.

"Mr. Stirling hit you last night. There is no way in hell I am letting you go back there without me." Colin's tone was stern.

"I'll be fine," I said, attempting to reassure him.

"I'm going, or you're not," he instructed, standing and leaving the room, removing all option for argument. I guess he was going.

CHAPTER 25

*A*t every turn there was a memory. Pulling up to the vast driveway, I remembered the strolls we would take outside of his parents' property. I also remembered an argument Ashton and I had in the car, just before a Sunday family dinner, during which I thought I might have to flee from his fury.

Climbing the stone steps, I recalled an image of the teenage Clementine, perched over Ashton's shoulder, watching him as he worked on his English paper. Just being in the same space as Ashton used to be enough to fill me up.

As I paused at the top of the stairs, I recalled a moment when Ashton's cousins were skipping across the oversized porch, leaping onto our laps on the hanging wooden swing. Ashton was always great with kids; I suppose it was a small blessing we never had any.

"You don't have to do this," Colin reminded me. Now that he had flown all this way with me, I was actually quite glad to have him by my side. The anxiety had begun to overwhelm me on the flight here. I didn't call ahead to let the Stirlings know I was coming, for fear I might lose my nerve. I hadn't even told my mother of my plans, who I knew, like Colin, would not approve.

"I know I don't have to," I said with a smile, and then glanced in the direction of the rental car. "Can you wait for me at the car?"

He hesitated before answering, "Em, what if something happens? I would feel better if I could keep my eyes on you. I need to know you're safe."

"I'm sure I'll be fine," I replied.

"I'll wait at the bottom of the steps, but you have to promise me if you feel at all uncomfortable, you'll call out to me," Colin instructed. "I'll be in there in a heartbeat."

"Fine, although I'm certain there won't be any need for that." I watched as Colin sulked down the stairs. Once at the bottom, he turned, looking up at me with wide eyes.

I took a deep breath and pressed the familiar button at the right of the doorframe, listening to the muffled chimes. When the hollow clicking noises of shoes against hardwood floors neared, my heart rate shot up, and I began to hear a popping noise in my ears. I didn't know what to expect when the door opened. Would Maggie shut it in my face? I had been her daughter-in-law for years, but since the death of her son, I had abandoned her, no word of where I had disappeared.

As the door pulled open, I was relieved it was not Mr. Stirling who answered. I saw Ashton's mother staring back at me. It was shocking to see how much she had changed over only a couple years. Her golden hair was consumed by grays, and the faint lines around her eyes and mouth had deepened. Her eyes appeared as if they were shining when she drank me in.

"Clementine, my dear." Her voice was pleasant and welcoming—I was now confused. She looked over my shoulder, catching a glimpse of Colin who I can only assume was staring back. "What are you doing here?"

"I'm sorry I didn't call, Maggie, I mean, Mrs. Stirling," I quickly corrected. I was sure she must loathe me, and my use of her first name must have made her sick.

"Nonsense, you don't ever need to call, and I'm always Maggie to you. Do you want to come in?" she asked, stepping to one side.

"Yes, thank you." I walked past her. The last time I had entered this home it was as their daughter-in-law, but I was surprised it felt the same.

"Your friend, would he like to come in?" Maggie asked looking down at him, a smile across her face. I was certain she was curious as to his identity.

"No," I quickly replied, in case Colin might have heard her suggestion and accepted the offer. "He's fine out there."

Maggie was well put together; she had always been that way. A skirt with a dark navy floral print tickled her ankles and a cream blouse that came together with a loose bow at the neck covered her torso. A circular brooch that was covered in rhinestones complimented her navy cardigan to top off her ensemble. Ashton bought jewelry for his mother for every holiday; it had always been a thing between them, and I knew she treasured each piece.

"Mag, who was at the door?" My back stiffened as soon as I heard Mr. Stirling's voice.

"Clementine has come for a visit dear," Maggie answered, ushering me into the formal living room. I peered around the room; it looked as though not a single thing had been disturbed since last I saw the place. On the mantle was Ashton's senior picture, and across from it, one from our wedding. Part of me was surprised Mr. Stirling hadn't insisted on removing it.

I could hear him coming closer, bounding through the house with his heavy footsteps. Bursting into the room he glared at me, the bruises from the altercation between him and Colin evident now. "What are you doing here, girl?"

"Robert!" Maggie scolded.

"I won't have this whore in my house, Maggie!" he replied sternly.

"You will be silent," Maggie commanded. I had never heard her speak to Mr. Stirling in such a tone. I honestly didn't think she had it in her. It was obvious there had been some changes since Ashton passed. "Clementine has come here to talk to us, and we will listen... do you understand?"

He didn't reply, but it was clear he was not pleased with the current circumstances. We all took a seat, and I struggled with where to begin.

"Would you like anything to drink, sweetie?" Maggie offered. I didn't dare look to Mr. Stirling, but I could feel his eyes. I wanted to do this and get out of there as quickly as possible.

"No, thank you, I'm fine," I replied.

"Very well," Maggie replied, crossing her hands delicately over her lap. "What brings you to our home today?"

"Actually, I wanted to talk to you, Maggie," I began.

"About what?" Mr. Stirling demanded, raising his voice slightly.

Part of me considered calling for Colin right then, but I knew I needed to get through this on my own. "What we discussed in New York, Mr. Stirling. I felt like she deserved to hear it directly from me."

"She deserved to hear it three years ago," he snapped.

"I agree, but—" I began, before Maggie interrupted me.

"What conversation in New York?" she questioned. My mouth fell open. How had he not told her everything that had happened? I couldn't fathom how he might have explained the bruise on his cheek.

"Nothing," Mr. Stirling replied quickly, hopping to his feet he began to pace like a caged animal.

"Child, you need to tell me everything," she instructed, not looking at her husband.

"No! I'm not going to let her come in here and spin her lies. There is nothing she could say that I think either of us should listen to. She wasn't there for our son, and when you needed her, she wasn't here for you either," Mr. Stirling said, stopping for the moment to talk to his wife.

"And you were? Darling," her tone was cool, as she directed her statement at Mr. Stirling, "I'll decide who was there for me and who wasn't. You can either sit down and remain silent, or leave the room."

Mr. Stirling gasped, and in a huff, exited the room, making his way through the dining area and into their kitchen, where he proceeded to slam the cabinets and make a general raucous.

"Don't mind him. Please, continue," she urged. I didn't

want to create any problems between Mr. and Mrs. Stirling. I could only imagine what their marriage had endured since Ashton had been taken from them. I would do my best to limit the damage.

"I came because I wanted to tell you about that night... the night Ashton—" I stopped. I couldn't say it, at least not to his mother.

"Killed himself." To my surprise, she did it for me.

"Yes, I'm sorry," I offered. She nodded, motioning for me to continue. "That night, I wasn't completely honest about everything, and the way it happened."

"In what way?" she asked, tilting her head inquisitively. Was this it? Had the time come where I was actually going to tell his mother that I could have prevented his death? Did I have the nerve to tell her I instead encouraged him?

"Maggie, you have to believe me, I didn't tell you a lot of this because I didn't want to change the way you looked at your son," I explained.

"I doubt anything you could say would change the way I look at Ashton," she replied. I wasn't sure if she meant that she was confident in her opinion of who he was, or that she thought of me as a liar. I decided not to dwell on the statement.

"Ashton and I had been having trouble in our marriage, almost since the beginning. We were trying—I mean, I didn't want our marriage to be over, but it had become so hard." From the way she was looking at me, I worried I wasn't conveying the story properly.

"Marriage can be hard. I know Ashton's father and I have struggled at times," Maggie offered. I felt even more like a hopeless disappointment in that moment. I knew

Mr. Stirling could be unbearable, yet somehow she had managed to make it work with the man all of these years. I gave up on her only child so quickly. I prepared myself for what was to come next—there was no way I could say this so that she would take it well. I was about to break her heart, and that's all there was to it.

"It felt like I had been trying for so long, but things weren't getting better. They were worse. I know I told everyone I found Ashton when I came home from the grocery store, but that's not how it happened." My voice began to quiver, and I thought I might not be able to go through with it.

Maggie scooted to the edge of her seat, leaning forward; she reached out and placed her hand on top of mine. Looking up at her, in those sympathetic grief filled eyes, a tear escaped, rolling down my cheek, and I heaved, struggling to control my breathing. "It's all right, I'm right here."

She was here, in the moment, at least she would be until I told her what a terrible person I was. She needed to know the truth, and I was about to give it to her, if I could just hold it together long enough. "I told him that night I was leaving—we were over. He begged me not to go. I should have listened to him; I never should have turned my back on him."

"I know how hard the Stirling men can be, Clementine. I'm sure had you known what was going to happen you would have been there."

Was there nothing I could say that would make this woman hate me? Yes, there was one thing. "He told me."

She furrowed her brow, her hand still on mine. From

the corner of my eye I could see Mr. Stirling standing in the doorway leading to the dining room, watching us. "Told you what?"

I dared not look up at Ashton's father, and instead kept my eyes trained on Maggie. "He told me if I left him he would kill himself. I told him to do what he had to do, but I was leaving."

"You see!" Mr. Stirling shouted, rushing over. "She's a murderer. We let her in our lives, we loved her like she was our daughter, and she repays us by killing our son."

There it was—that was the reaction I had expected; yet from Maggie I still got nothing. She sat there with a blank stare.

"I'm so sorry," I whispered, unable to hold back the onslaught of tears, letting them flow freely down my cheeks.

"You're sorry? She's sorry!" Mr. Stirling shouted. "Sorry doesn't bring Ashton back to us. What we should do is call the police right now. You should be in jail, that's where you should be."

I dropped my head in shame. Perhaps he was right.

"Robert," Maggie spoke again at last, choosing her words carefully. "I won't ask you again to be silent."

"What? Me?" he cried, staring at his wife in disbelief.

"Yes, you! Ashton was your son through and through. Why do you think he drank so much? His father was an alcoholic. Why would he have been anything different? Our son had his problems, before he ever met Clementine, and it is not fair for you to put all of that on this poor girl," Maggie condemned her husband.

"How dare—" he began.

"How dare nothing!" Maggie snapped. "You know the things I'm saying are true. We'll talk about this later."

He turned on his heel, darting up the stairs, outraged by the confrontation.

"I'm sorry you had to see that. The past few years have been particularly hard on Ashton's father," Maggie explained. I didn't know if I should hug her for her kindness or shake her and ask why she wasn't screaming at me. "I have something of my own I should have shared with you a long time ago. I suppose for not telling you, I somewhat blame myself for what happened."

"Oh no, Mrs. Stirling—I mean, Maggie. Don't ever say that."

"It's a mad world, Clementine—one that my son always had trouble wrapping his brain around. When he was thirteen he tried to kill himself. And then again at fourteen. Pills. He should have told you. I should have told you. He was so different when he met you. He was happy for a change. Looking back now, I think he hid his secret misery from us, but I can see now what he must have put you through." Maggie's eyes shifted to the mantle and the picture of Ashton. "It wasn't fair to put that on you. You should have known what you were getting yourself into."

"Maggie," I said in a barely audible tone.

"I know. I'm so sorry, child," she offered. I didn't want her apologies. I didn't know what I wanted except to put all of this behind me. I didn't understand how the past could stop all of our lives—none of us able to move forward.

"Please don't say you're sorry. I was the one who should have said something that night. I'm sorry," I repeated. "Maybe your husband is right, and I should go to jail for this. I feel like I should be punished."

"I can tell you've been punishing yourself for a very long time. I think you've put yourself through enough," she stated, standing and reaching for me to join her.

I rose to my feet, still a little shaky. Wrapping her arms around me she pulled me into an embrace. When at last she released me, all I could think to say was, "Thank you."

She walked me to the door, and after opening it, she peered out and looked down at Colin. She smiled and waved to him. Awkwardly, he waved back. Leaning in she whispered, "He's very handsome."

I blushed in response. "I don't know how I can thank you, Maggie. I never thought you would be so understanding."

"Clementine, I would give anything to have my Ashton back. I also would have given anything for him to be able to accept love. He was lost, and I was his mother and couldn't bring him back from the edge. I believe Ashton loved us—I have to. And because of that, I have decided he wouldn't want us to carry these scars. If my kindness lets you take them off your back, then I'm happy, because I think it's what Ashton wanted to do for you, but couldn't."

My eyes swollen and cheeks wet, I threw my arms around her again. I squeezed as tightly as I could, wishing somehow I could make her scars fade a little.

"I know," she replied as I released her. "Don't be a stranger. I miss you."

"Okay, I'll call," I replied, surprising even myself that I meant it.

Walking down the stairs I caught Colin's eyes, his

brows arched in anticipation, his hand outstretched toward me. Looking over my shoulder back at Maggie, and back at the life that had once trapped me, I sighed, waving goodbye. I just hoped one day Mr. Stirling could be as forgiving as his wife.

As my fingertips met Colin's, my heart fluttered. A hope and relief I hadn't ever felt consumed me. We neared the car, and he asked, "Well?"

"It went well," I replied.

"I'm going to need more than that," he pushed.

"I have somewhere else I want to go," I said, ignoring his prompting.

"Where?" he asked, opening my door for me.

"You'll see." I smiled, wondering if it was possible to even do what Maggie said. Now that I had these scars, would I ever be able to have them removed?

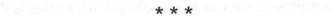

CHAPTER 26

I stared at the grass on the front lawn, a couple inches longer than it should be. There was a small plastic red toy car with a yellow roof turned over on its side near the bottom of the driveway. The garage door had been painted from taupe to a bright white, and the siding was replaced with a bright yellow color. I couldn't help but wonder if it was done in an effort to mask the sadness the place contained.

"Are you going to tell me why we're here, or are we just going to continue to play creepy stalker couple?" Colin asked.

"Not yet," I answered. I wasn't ready to explain to him what this place was. I wanted a future with him, and here we were, staring at the place that held so much of my past.

Frustrated, Colin flipped on the radio, thumbing through the stations until finally settling on one. I didn't know why we were here, or why I wanted to see this place. I wanted to move on, I wanted to do what Maggie told me and let my scars fade, but it seemed impossible. I

don't think she was right about Ashton loving me. I think
he killed himself because he wanted me to hurt. It seemed
like a disservice to him if I were to let go of the pain.

"Oh me, oh my, oh, look at Miss Ohio," Colin sang
from the driver's seat. I glanced over at him and smiled.
"She's a-running around with her rag-top down."

"What are you doing?" I asked, laughing lightly.

"She says I wanna do right, but not right now," he
continued.

"Stop it, Colin," I commanded. I didn't want him to
sing. I wanted to wallow in self-pity, and that was impossible with him singing.

Turning the volume down, he said, "No, I won't stop
singing unless you tell me what we're doing here."

"I'm not ready to talk about it," I explained, looking
away from him and back at the home.

"Well, I am, and I'm here, and I want to know what
we're doing," Colin added in a more demanding tone.

Looking at him, contempt heavy in my stare, I growled
back, "That's too bad. We can't always get what we want
and you have to learn that."

He reached over, gripping my leg in an effort to hold
my attention. "Em, I'm here. I want to take this from you,
which is why I came. I'm in love with you, damn it, let me
be there for you."

My heart ached to the point that I wondered if it
might turn to ash within my chest. I couldn't conceive
how such beautiful words could hurt so much. "You can't
take it from me."

He looked over my shoulder at the silent home. "Was
that where it happened?"

I nodded, relieved he knew where we were, and I didn't have to say the words. The car began to feel quite small, and I struggled to catch my breath. Colin did his best to calm me, although his efforts were useless. I leapt from the vehicle as if I were leaping from my own coffin. Colin exited, too, standing and staring at me from across the car. I turned and peered at the house.

"I swear, Em, if you leave me I'll kill myself." I remembered the way those words sounded that night. I could see now, the way he said it, he was trying to tell me he was looking for a way to be done. I wondered if he was asking for permission. *"I'm not kidding, I'll do it! I can't live without you."* Was he right? Was that why he did it? If that was why he did it then maybe he really did love me… he needed me to keep going. It felt like my mind was spinning.

Turning on my heel I looked to Colin, who hadn't taken his eyes from me. "Can we go to his grave?"

He nodded, sadness in his eyes. I was certain this must have felt like torture to him, but I couldn't help myself. He wanted to be there, and I needed closure. He replied in a soft voice, "Whatever you need."

* * *

The flowers on the grave were fresh, and I could see Maggie had taken great care in making sure they stayed that way. The image of the guitar on the tombstone made me smile. I hadn't seen the grave since the day of his funeral, when there was no actual stone to look at. I never told his family, I let them assume I would visit. My mother placed flowers for me that first year. Seeing his tombstone with his name was more than I thought I could ever handle. But now, being here, I realized I was stronger than I thought.

"You loved him, didn't you?" Colin asked. There was no jealousy in his voice, only sorrow. I worried it might hurt him to know the truth, but I was too tired to lie anymore.

"Yes. In a lot of ways, I guess I did," I replied.

Colin put his arm around my shoulder. I felt like I should pull away—that somehow it was disrespectful to Ashton, but it felt so comforting, I couldn't. "Sometimes love isn't enough. It's not your fault."

"I'm so tired of people saying that. It is my fault. He needed me, and I basically told him to go screw himself." I couldn't help but be agitated. I wasn't mad at Colin; I was angrier with Ashton and myself. It wasn't fair he didn't tell me about his attempts to kill himself as a kid. I was his wife. I should have known that.

"What do you want me to do? Do you want me to lie? I don't think it was your fault. I want to make this better, so why won't you let me?"

"You can't make this better, Colin! Stop trying! This will never be better, and if you're not all right with that, then you might want to move on now!" I yelled, not taking my eyes from Ashton's grave.

Colin pulled away. He was silent; I couldn't even hear his breathing anymore. I heard the earth rustling as he turned and walked away. I glanced over my shoulder. I was nervous he might be leaving me at the gravesite, not that I would blame him. He didn't. Instead, he stopped, leaning back against the car, arms crossed, head down.

Stepping closer, I got down onto my knees, the moist ground soaking through the denim. "Hi Ashton." It was odd talking to him. I had done it alone, in my room, or lying on the couch at my mother's, but to be here, knowing he was in the earth beneath me, it felt like he might be able to hear me.

"That's Colin. I hope you're not angry, but we're dating. Well, we were, but I probably screwed that up, too. I think the curse of us is probably too much for any man." I sat quietly for a second, a numbness coming over me. "Ashton, I don't understand why."

My voice began to shake, tears slipping from my eyes. "You had to know it would destroy me, your mother... God, your dad, he's a mess, Ash. Did you hate us all that much?"

A breeze blew through the trees above as a chill overwhelmed me, causing my entire body to shiver. In that instant I had an overwhelming desire to curl up on Ashton's grave, cover myself in dead leaves creating a blanket, and use the tombstone as a pillow. I would stay there, mourning him, for eternity.

A warm hand grazed my cheek just before it touched my shoulder. Looking up, for a split second, part of me expected to see Ashton. Colin looked down at me instead. He had snuck up on me—he was good at that. Taking his hand, I sighed and brushed my knees off as I stood. He didn't speak, only wrapped his arms around me in the warmest embrace. We lingered until at last he released me, guiding me back to the car.

He didn't open the door, he didn't say a word, he only stood there, blocking my path and looking at me.

"Is everything okay?" I asked, looking away, trying to clean up my tear stained cheeks.

"I don't know," he replied, and I braced myself for what I assumed was the break up talk.

"I understand," I replied softly.

"No, you don't, and that's the problem," Colin said, his voice shaking slightly.

I looked up at him, his eyes moist, but no tears. "What?"

"Let me get through this before you say anything," he began. I swallowed hard, preparing for the goodbye. "You know that scar on your chin? It's the most beautiful looking scar I have ever seen. I love that when you say you want black coffee you really mean you want one sugar. Your smile, your style, and all the things about you that make you into the girl I love are among my favorite things in this world. I still remember the look on your face when we first met, that disgust for the warehouse, not to mention me. It makes me feel alive to think of those things. I need you, Em. Without you my heart would break."

"Don't say that!" I exclaimed, a flash of Ashton's plea playing in my mind.

"I have to say it. I'm sorry your husband did what he did. I wish I understood it. But honestly, I can't, because with or without you, the only place I want to be is in a world you're a part of. If I lost you, I would fight every day to have you back. I wouldn't do something I know would hurt you. I love you too much for that. I may not be able to eat or sleep, but I would go on breathing if it meant one day I might have you back. I wish he had loved you enough to not hurt you, but he did hurt you. I would never do that to you, Em, and all I ask is that you give me every day to try and take a little bit of the pain away that he caused."

"Damn it, Colin," I mumbled through the stream of tears.

He laughed, scooping me into his embrace. "Does that mean you won't leave me."

I nodded. He lifted my chin, wiping away my tears with his thumbs as he gripped my face.

"I thought you were going to break up with me after this trip," I confessed.

"What?" he scoffed. "Never. It took too much work to catch you just to throw you back."

"Nice..." I huffed.

Leaning closer his lips met mine; it felt like he was kissing the pain, numbing it for now. Pulling away he stepped to the side, allowing me to slide in. I looked toward the grave one last time. "Goodbye," I whispered, hoping I might be able to leave the ghost behind that had been haunting me for the past few years. Colin made his way around the car, taking his proper place next to me.

CHAPTER 27

"Your eyes are closed?" Colin yelled from across the room.

"Yes," I replied impatiently. "I told you they were before I even came in."

"Okay, hang on." I could hear Colin's footsteps bounding toward me. In a few seconds his warm hand took hold of mine, my fingertips brushing over the bandaid on his pinky. "This way... just hold my hand and follow my voice. A little closer... we're almost there. All right."

He halted and I stumbled slightly. "Can I open them?"

"Oh yeah, sorry, open your eyes."

I actually gasped when I did. The room was open and bright, the new furniture complementing the industrial feel. "Oh Colin, it's amazing!"

"Look behind you," he instructed, pointing over my shoulder. Hanging over a bench on the main wall, just before you entered the master bedroom was my painting. I painted it after our trip to Ohio and called it 'The flowers in her hair' after The Lumineers' song. A woman began in the fetal position, and in the painting you could see the motion of her standing, and leaping high, a few flowers in her hair.

"Wow, right in the entry, you must like it." I smiled.

"Not just me," Colin grinned, his arms wrapping around me and coming to rest at my lower back.

"What do you mean?" I asked, puzzled.

"The investor I've been talking to was here today. He said he loved it. It was pretty amazing to tell him my girlfriend painted it," Colin explained.

"Wait! What? Back up!" I exclaimed. "You had an investor here? What did he say about the place? Did you show him the master bath? I mean, that is amazing... you had to have shown him. Right? And the kitchen, now that the marble is in... it's perfection. Are you going to tell me what he said?"

"If you let me get a word in." Colin laughed.

"Sorry," I said, lifting my hand up to my mouth and pressing firmly.

Colin pulled it away, kissing my fingers. "Well, he said the last minute decision to change out the concrete and add the wood floors was definitely the way to go."

"Well, duh, any moron can see that," I snapped. Colin stared at me, lifting his eyebrows. "Sorry, keep going."

"He told me it's obvious I have an understanding of what high end buyers are looking for." Colin paused, his eyes not shifting from me.

"And?" I pushed.

"And... he would be happy to go into business with me. I've got the funding," Colin said, his mouth hanging open, waiting for my response. I squealed, a wave of pure excitement washing over me. Colin lifted me off the ground hugging me so tightly I thought for a moment he might crack my spine.

He set me down, the bliss of the moment washing over us both. "You did an amazing job, Colin—you really should be proud. Although, my paintings do make the space look that much more fantastic."

"Is that right?" Colin laughed.

"Yes, I mean, I think so," I replied, flashing a mischievous grin.

"I happen to agree, and so does your professor. Which is why we need to get moving or we will be late for your show opening," Colin reminded me, placing his hand on the small of my back, and ushering me toward the door.

"Paige and Christian will be there for sure?" I inquired, my head now swimming with excitement.

"That's what he told me," Colin reaffirmed.

I twisted my body as we neared the door causing Colin to stop. He glared at me with a puzzled gaze. "Hold on."

"What is it?" Colin asked, a nervous tremor in his voice. I wasn't surprised after everything I had put him through in the recent months. The on-again off-again status had to be hard on him. After we got home from Ohio, the break up conversations ended, but I think he still worried I might relapse, slipping back into the suit of despair I had grown accustomed to for all those years.

I closed the space between us, my face hovering only inches from his. My body began to move with his breathing. I slipped my arms around his body, clasping them together at his waist. He leaned back slightly, pulling his face away and looking down at me, a slight smile on his lips.

"I wanted to take a second, together, before tonight. I know it will probably be crazy," I explained, my cheek warm from his breath as he sighed in relief.

"I want you to know something, Em. I think you know I wasn't looking for this when we met, and honestly, I never thought something like what we have would find me, but—"

"I know," I interrupted. Colin always felt like he needed to tell me how special I was to him. Ashton had always done the same thing—a lot of words to say how amazing I was. But that was the thing—they were just words. Colin was different. "You show me everyday, babe. I know."

"Move in with me!" he blurted out, staring into my eyes for some sort of response.

I hesitated, shocked by the statement. At last I asked, "What about Paige? I can't do that to her."

"This isn't spur of the moment. I was going to ask you later tonight, after the show, but I can't wait. I already talked to Paige and Christian, and they said they would be happy to live together at your place, and you can move in here with me.

My heart started racing. I couldn't believe what I was hearing. I didn't take my eyes from him as he took a stray strand of hair and tucked it behind my ear. I leaned forward and kissed his chin, then the spot just to the right of his smile.

Pulling away, he gazed into my eyes, slipping his hands up to my cheeks, cradling my face. "Is that a yes?"

I nodded, all the hair on my neck standing up. "Yes, Colin Bennett, I'll move in with you." He knew me. That was obvious. If it were up to him he would be proposing marriage, but he knew me. He loved me for all of my broken pieces, and he was willing to put all of them back together one by one, for as long as it took. It may have taken time, and it was definitely a stubborn love. But it was real. And it was ours.

READ PAIGE'S STORY NOW

ONLY IN DREAMS

My tone surprises him. He looks me in my eyes and says, "I guess it's true. A guy like me only gets the girl in his dreams."

When he walks out the door I turn and collapse into a chair, clutching the tattoo on my wrist. I just might take the chance. Weezer's "Only In Dreams," begins to play in my head as if on repeat. I grab the towel on the back of the chair next to me and press it to my face, comforting myself. It's over, don't cry for him, it's finally over. He has to hate you after that. - Only In Dreams

Emmie Hayes' best friend, Paige has created a life for herself. She's finally happy, that is until Christian Bennett resurfaces. Suddenly she learns doing the thing that is right for your soul isn't always the easiest for your heart.

* Contains mature content including death, romantic situations, and some mature language.

PREVIEW OF ONLY IN DREAMS

I LOOK AT the clock again. I'm not sure what secrets I expect it to reveal. I've looked at it at least a hundred times in the last hour. 3:46 AM. Next, I look at my phone. This has become my ritual this evening. I have somehow become the girl I swore I would never be—the one waiting at home for the phone to ring.

When Christian and I moved in together three months ago, I thought the things that had been haunting him would somehow disappear. But, if anything, he has gotten worse. Even Emmie knows something is wrong. Though she does her best not to flaunt her and Colin's love fest in my face, I can't help but look at them and be reminded of all the things that are wrong between Christian and myself.

I've tried talking to him about his behavior. I tell him I can see that he's hurting; this approach only makes him angry. I know he's been drinking again, but every time I try and discuss it, he tells me to quit mothering him. Christ, I'm twenty-two years old. I shouldn't have to worry about this stuff. Yet here I am. I look back at the clock. *Damn it Christian, where are you?*

The most horrible and terrifying things a person can imagine have been going through my mind. I've tried calling his cell several times, but now the mailbox is full. I mean, come on, a full mailbox? He would be furious if I treated him this way. When my agent called me earlier today and told me about an opportunity in Paris to model I turned him down flat. But now, with each passing minute that Christian disrespects me, without so much as a call, I am reconsidering my choice.

I love him; I know that much. And I used to be pretty sure he loved me. All of my model friends float from guy to guy and can't seem to understand what Christian and I have. It just doesn't make sense to them. Of course, it's not making very much sense to me either right now.

My mom was always in competition with me. First, with my dad, she would do everything she could to make sure he saw me as worthless. Eventually he couldn't stand being around her anymore. That was when she tried to use me as a weapon against him. I never blamed him, or maybe it was just that I no longer cared enough anymore about either of them to give a damn. But when my mom started making fun of me and telling all her boyfriends what a loser I was, I decided I wanted to be anywhere except in her house.

Then Christian walked into to my life. I wasn't looking for a man to rescue me; I was never that kind of girl. No, the great thing about him was that he was just as messed up and broken from the death of his parents, but somehow, we made sense together. At first we partied, and then when Christian realized after graduation that he didn't seem to know when to stop drinking, we simply fell into our next phase of life together. We could go out with all our friends, and because we had each other, Christian never needed to get wasted. He just liked being near me.

I'm not kidding myself. For the most part, I know he has always been about himself. He likes to look good, he likes to hang out with a certain crowd and attend the important events. When life gets to be too much you can find him at the gym, working on his massive muscles. Even Colin, his brother, is constantly teasing him about his manscaping. But even though he likes himself a lot, he's always managed to make me feel important and loved … until now.

I know if I could just get through to him, figure out what's causing all of these feelings he has been having, I could help him. But … I hear the key in the lock. I shift in my seat multiple times, unsure how I should handle this confrontation. My heart begins to race. Without thinking, I leap from the chair I am perched in and flop onto the couch, laying down with my eyes closed.

What am I doing? I think. *Am I really going to pretend like I'm asleep? Apparently so.*

I hear the door open, and Christian grunts as he fumbles with the lock, trying to remove his keys. Once the door is closed I listen for the lock to latch, but it doesn't happen. Instead I hear footsteps stumbling toward me—dragging across the floor. From the smell assaults my senses, I can tell he is extremely intoxicated.

I wait silently, assuming he's now staring at me, but I can't be sure. It's too late not to continue with the charade. Then I hear more footsteps, and the bedroom door bash into the wall. Quickly I sit up and turn around, watching Christian stumble into the guest room. I can't believe what I'm seeing. Why on Earth would he be going in there?

I've had enough of the game. I want answers. I deserve answers. I hop to my feet and rush across the living room, poking my head in through the doorway Christian passed through moments ago. He is passed out, still fully dressed, including his shoes. Lying sideways across the bed, drool leaks from his mouth.

"Seriously?" is the only thing I can think to say. I want to cry; I want to throw things at him, and scream horrible things at him. But I don't do that. The last time I cried was when my dad left, and I decided nobody would ever get to see me do that again.

Christian mumbles an inaudible response, which then trails off into a snore.

"Christian? You've got to be kidding me." I try again, but I know he won't be waking up. Our talk will have to wait until morning. Unfortunately, sleep won't come as easily for me.

* * *

THE HOURS TICK by, and just as I suspected I've been unable to sleep. I lay in our bed at first, my face growing hot with anger. Then I clean, but I hate cleaning, so that doesn't last long. I think about calling Emmie around six o'clock, but that seems whiney and desperate. Not to mention the fact that I know most of what I tell Emmie she will tell Colin. If Colin knows Christian is getting wasted every night, it will start a huge fight between them, just giving him more ammo to use against me.

No, this is my problem, and I need to deal with it. By seven, I have come to the conclusion that maybe Christian isn't taking me seriously. I am always happy to clean up his messes, and it seems that he is well aware of it. Maybe now what he needs is some tough love. Maybe he needs to know I'm not going to be taken for granted anymore.

I waffle on this decision for sometime—I'm not one for idle threats—and before I make the ultimatum, I need to be certain I'll follow through. Poking my head into the guest bedroom one last time is all it takes. The room smells like a distillery. I realize now I love him enough to leave.

Packing my suitcase is harder than I thought it would be. I keep telling myself, *he won't let you leave, seeing your packed bags will be enough*. Going through the drawers, one by one, folding up my favorite thrift store treasures or photo shoot take home items, my mind drifts to Emmie.

She was a wreck when I met her. She didn't have any friends and was clearly suffering when it came to her fashion sense. I was the one who encouraged her to see how things would turn out with Colin. I was the example of happiness ... wasn't I? How did I end up here? I missed my last two modeling jobs because Christian needed one thing or another. Now my agent had warned me that the calls would stop coming if I didn't start putting my best foot forward.

I gather the essential hair and makeup products I cannot live without and strategically place my suitcases against the wall, so that Christian will see them first thing when he wakes up. Then I wait, and wait, until I refuse to wait any longer.

Grabbing a wad of cash and my keys, I shove them into the pockets of my jumper and head to Ninth Street Espresso to grab a coffee. After a night of no sleep I need it, especially if I am going to have anything left in me for the shit storm that I know is going to happen when I get home. I keep having these moments where I think perhaps I'm overreacting, but as I recall the recent months, I quickly dismiss these notions.

"Hey Bill," I grumble as I approach the counter.

"Paige, where's Christian this fine morning?"

I debate how to answer. Christian and Colin are the owners of the space the coffee shop rents. While a huge part of me wants to unload on Bill and tell him exactly where Christian is, and exactly what my boyfriend can do to himself, I worry how this might affect their business relationship.

"Sleeping in." I decide to play it safe.

"Boy, he's got it rough, doesn't he?" Bill laughs. I feign a smile as I watch him prepare my latte.

"New tat?" I inquire, trying not to think about my good-for-nothing sloth of a boyfriend who is still passed out at home.

"How can you possibly notice that? Besides my girl-friend, you're the only one," Bill marvels, handing me my cup. Bill has tattooed sleeves on both arms; it is something I always take notice of while he makes my drinks. I've always been fascinated with body art—tattoos being a permanent fashion statement.

I pull out the wad of bills from my pocket, even though I already know Bill is going to wave me off. "On the house," he says.

I couldn't explain it to him. I had been taking free coffee from this place for as long as I could remember. And until today it was merely one of the perks of dating an owner of the building, but now, it feels dirty. I am so angry at Christian, the free coffee perk has become an unimaginable sin.

'No, I insist, you always give me freebies. I think we should start a policy where I at least pay for one out of a hundred," I joke, shoving the money further onto the counter.

"Your money is no good here, you know that," Bill replies lifting his hands up into the air.

Grabbing the wadded up bills, I drop them into the tip jar and walk out, flashing a smile over my shoulder. Bill is nice; it is too bad his landlord is such a dick head.

The walk home is the longest walk I have ever taken. I'm more than fine if it takes me the rest of the morning to get home. But, even with dragging my feet, a short fifteen minutes later, here I am, staring at the front door of my building.

I really do love this place, the ivy has begun to climb across the brick, and I am so thrilled I convinced Colin not to cut it back. The window boxes are overflowing with the springtime flowers I recently planted. As I fiddle with the keys, small rays of sunshine filter through the leaves of the big oak tree that is bursting from the seams of the green space on the sidewalk.

This place is home—one of the few places in my life that I feel like nobody can take away from me. Now that Christian and I live together, we can never undo the choice. He owns the building, so if anyone is going to move out, it is going to be me.

I shake my head, trying to force the idea out of my mind. There is no way it is going to come to that, I remind myself. Even if I left for a few days, Christian will realize how miserable he is without me, and I will be back —back in his arms. And not the arms of the guy passed out in the guest room. I'll be back with my Christian, the one I fell in love with as a teen.

I climb the stairs and enter the apartment. Looking around, I quickly realize Christian still isn't awake. I huff and push the wild strands of hair out of my face. I've waited long enough. This needs to happen.

Stepping into the guest room, I clear my throat, loudly. Christian lay in the exact same position as the night before, clearly undisturbed by my presence. Angrily, I rush over to his oversized, beefy body and give him multiple shoves. "Wake up. You need to wake up, now!"

"Huh," he says with a snort, wiping the drool gathering on his cheek with the back of his hand. "What's going on?"

He seems startled. He lifts his eyes, and squinting, tries to block out the light more with his hand.

"We need to talk," I say coolly.

I watch as he rolls his eyes and flops back down onto

the bed, clearly disgusted I woke him. "Can't this wait?" he moans.

"It has waited, all morning," I reply firmly.

"Paige, I'm serious, I feel like crap."

"That's not my fault."

"Jesus! I said not right now."

"Don't you dare raise your voice to me," I command, completely in shock that he would have the nerve to talk to me that way after putting me through hell last night. "For all I knew you were dead last night."

"I left my phone in Pete's car," Christian defends himself, not bothering to lift his head.

The answer does not appease me, only further infuriating me. "Pete Hannigan? The loser you said you were never going to see again, because all he does is hang out with a bunch of roadie losers at Kings and get drunk all the time? That Pete?"

"Yeah, that Pete!" Christian shouts, suddenly sitting up and glaring at me. I watch as he clutches his head, the sudden adjustment to his body and light obviously causing an intense pain. I'm not too ashamed to admit, I kind of feel he has it coming.

"What's going on with you?" I beg, fighting the urge to rush up and start shaking him wildly.

"Nothing," he grunts, standing and pushing past me to make his way into the bathroom. I walk into the living room, taking a seat on the chair that faces the door. He will have to look at me when he comes out. He will have to give me the answers I deserve.

I hear the flush, then a few seconds later he emerges from the doorway. He doesn't look at me, though. He makes his way to the kitchen sink and sticks his head under the faucet. After a good soaking, he lifts up, and while dripping water all over the floor, proceeds to question, "Where are the migraine pills?"

"Basket on the top of the fridge," I answer. I don't even know why. I have all this anger and fight inside of me, but all of the sudden I feel incredibly overwhelmed with sadness. He really doesn't care if I am upset. Perhaps I've been fooling myself about who he really is. As a girl I would watch my mom date these slime balls who would use her up until they were done and then throw her away. My stomach sinks as the idea I am exactly the same as her hits me.

"It's like a freaking jackhammer in my skull," he moans as he fidgets with the childproof cap, growing angrier.

I can't explain exactly what clicks for me in that moment. I stand and glide into the kitchen casually, grabbing the bottle from his hands, and pop the lid off with ease. I deal out a dose, replace the lid, and turn to pick up my bags.

"Where are you going?" he asks, noticing the luggage for the first time.

"I'm leaving," I say and make my way to the door, but before I can get there, he takes hold of my arm.

"Where? A job?" I can see it in his eyes. He knows what is happening as much as I do, but his voice almost sounds hopeful it really is just a modeling job.

"Yeah," I reply. I don't intend on taking the job in Paris, but when he asks me the question, the reply just slips out.

"When will you be back?" he inquires, his eyes shifting from my bags and then to my face repeatedly.

"I'm not coming back," I answer, a sigh of relief passing my lips. This isn't at all how I had expected the talk to go. I planned to complain and tell him how miserable I am. I would demand he change, or I would move out. But standing at the door, this isn't the tone at all. Christian is the kind of broken that I can't fix—he needs to fix himself.

"What the hell do you mean?" He is clearly becoming agitated very quickly.

"You know this has been coming for a long time. You need help, and I hope you get it, but I can't sit here and watch you self-destruct. I love you too much for that. I can feel the rush of emotions building up, but I know this goodbye can't be emotional, or it will scar both of us more than we can handle.

"Are you kidding me? I party too hard with the boys, I don't check in, and you're done."

"I—"

"I don't want to hear it, Paige. I'm sick of the drama. Get out then, if you're leaving, just leave," Christian snaps before turning his back to me.

I've never felt two such conflicting emotions at the same time. Part of me can see he is hurting. I want to scoop him up into my arms, pull him in close, and make it better. But then there is another part of me that loud and clear is telling myself, you deserve more than your mom and dad, you deserve more than him.

And then it happens, I says the words, "Goodbye, Christian." The door closes behind me, my first love on one side, the rest of my life on the other.

* * *

ACKNOWLEDGMENTS

Thank you to the many bloggers who are on the front lines every day, helping authors like me reach readers. I can't thank you enough for what you do.

Thank you to my editor, Madison Seidler. You put up with my incessant rambling, questions, blatant misspellings, and basically allowed me to pester the living hell out of you. Without your feedback and hard work this book wouldn't be what it is. Thanks as well for the final read through Chelsea.

To my husband, who helped me with my Stubborn Heart. Without him this book would not exist. He made several late night trips to grocery to get me five hour energy or my coffee fix, he played Mr. Mom on the weekends to allow me the time I needed to write, and his encouragement kept me going when self-doubt crept in. Most of all he was the one who helped me learn that I could love again after divorce.

For my three beautiful children: I lost track of how many times Mommy said she needed quiet time to write, but you all always did your best to oblige me, even if you didn't always succeed. During this book I discovered you are amazing at helping with chores, and I should have started you all cleaning years ago apparently. Seriously, though, all three of you were the best helpers any mommy could ever ask for. I love you all to the moon and back.

ABOUT THE AUTHOR

Wendy Owens was raised in the small college town of Oxford, Ohio. After attending Miami University, Wendy went on to a career in the visual arts. After several years of creating and selling her own artwork, she gave her first love, writing, a try.

Wendy now happily spends her days writing though she still enjoys painting. When she's not writing, she can be found spending time with her tech geek husband and their three amazing kids.

For More Information:
https://wendyowensbooks.com
me@wendyowensbooks.com
ALSO BY WENDY OWENS...

**Find links to all of Wendy's Books at
wendyowensbooks.com/books/**

PSYCHOLOGICAL THRILLER

My Husband's Fiancée (book1)
My Wife's Secrets (book 2)

The Day We Died
An Influential Murder

Secrets At Meadow Lake

COZY MYSTERIES
Jack Be Nimble, Jack Be Dead
O Deadly Night
Roses Are Red, Violet is Dead

YA ROMANCE
Wash Me Away

CONTEMPORARY ROMANCE (adult)
Stubborn Love
Only In Dreams
The Luckiest
Do Anything
It Matters to Me

YA PARANORMAL (clean)
Sacred Bloodlines
Unhallowed Curse
The Shield Prophecy
The Lost Years
The Guardians Crown

* * *